EUPHORIA

ANGELA NICOLE

This book is dedicated to the child that I was. The one that dreamed of becoming an author one day. And to all the people that supported me through this process. I am thankful for the part that every one of you played in my story.

Trigger warnings

Possible triggers within this novel:
Forced sexual encounters
Strong language
Implied abuse of various types

1

Olivia was saddened as she noticed a malnourished, scrappy-looking black kitten wandering through the empty parking lot of the local grocery store, looking for scraps where trash, needles, and pill baggies littered the ground. This had once been a beautiful and prosperous town. Her heart went out the small creature, wishing that she could save it from a life on the streets.

A loud cracking noise broke the silence, causing Olivia to gasp and jump back. Looking down, she realized that she had just stepped on a used syringe, most likely used for the current popular drug Ink. Thankfully, the needle had missed penetrating her foot through the soles of her new running shoes, purchased for times like these, when she had to walk miles through towns to assess the direness of the Ink epidemic. Their group helped to decide if towns, villages, and cities qualified to receive some form of aid to help clean up their streets and buildings.

The small group of officials from the task force looked on knowing that if they wandered around behind the store, they would be likely to find a few people passed out near the dumpsters, taking shelter in their drugged or drunken states in the early hours of the morning.

"It must be difficult to see your hometown falling to pieces like this, Liv," Sari commented, looking around with analytical eyes.

Olivia sighed, knowing that Sari was always searching for answers, for the how and the why. "Yes, it is hard to see Cital run-down like this. A lot of things seem to have changed since I left. I'm just glad my parents have retired and moved away."

"The epidemic is everywhere. Hopefully they're someplace that is less riddled with Ink."

"They are in a gated retirement community in the south. Warm weather and golf. That's all they want," she spoke softly. "All my ties to this place are long gone." Her coworker Dave could see the sorrow in Olivia created by the fall of this once prosperous, lively town. He tried to catch her eye, to send her a sign that he understood and wanted to help, that he cared.

She never noticed, her focus on the black kitten, watching where it went until it reached the corner of the building and disappeared, thinking that maybe she needed a pet to keep her company at night when it occasionally got lonely. With a sigh Olivia walked on, searching the landscape for other signs of hardship.

Continuing their tour of the town, they took note of the paraphernalia that littered the ground, any area that addicts seemed to congregate, and jotted the information down on the assessment form. It housed the typical demographic information for the town so that they were able to calculate risk and need. Olivia counted no less than twenty baggies and a handful of used needles in a five-block radius. After a couple more hours of walking and observing they headed for the downtown district to a little diner that served the best small-town meals in a fifty-mile radius, or so they had heard.

If I only look up at the sky and the tops of the trees, I can almost pretend that nothing is wrong here. There was a light breeze blowing through the trees, which were such a pretty green, so healthy and seemingly vital. The houses stood tall and were well cared for in this section of the city and yet needles and baggies still littered the ground. She knew that it would be an entirely different picture if she headed east, across to the other side of town, to the wrong side of the railroad tracks, so to speak. There she would find filth and decay, would see the sadness coming from the eyes of children, who had such a small chance of breaking the cycle that they had been forced to live in.

"Something needs to be done! We see this in every town, village, and city that we get called to survey," Olivia exclaimed.

Dave sighed deeply. "What can we do? We can't force everyone to stop doing drugs. Hell, new types are coming out every day, it seems."

Olivia scrunched up her face. "I just hate seeing my hometown in such a shamble. It is so damn sad. It gets worse with each step I take through this place. I don't understand how these people keep living like this."

A feeling of helplessness in that moment coursed through her as she silently vowed to herself and to the people of the town that she would find a way to make their world a better place. She may not have much say over the national government, but she knew that she had strong ties to the regional hierarchy.

Dave reached out to Olivia, taking hold of her hand reassuringly, brushing his thumb over her knuckles. It was a gentle touch, a soft and comforting touch, but those stroking fingers created an uncomfortable knot in her stomach. She thought back to a time when another person had held her hand like this, and how the sweeping movement of fingers had excited her so quickly, stirring desire low in her belly. She shook her head as though to physically remove the unwanted thoughts and quickly removed her hand from Dave's grasp.

Olivia walked on, more determined than ever to come up with a solution to offer a clean slate to those that wanted to live, work, be safe, and be clean. Had she been looking up while walking, or at least not so lost in thought, she may have had a small clue as to what she was about to walk into. The group, led by Olivia, rounded the corner and then they all fell back, gasping in shock at the picture that had spread out before them.

The house was a demure beige in color with maroon, hunter green, and dark brown accents. The window treatments were of the highest quality, and the front porch looked so inviting, as though it were saying, come sit and have a glass of lemonade and chat for a while. The furniture on the porch was built for comfort and was so immaculate, just as the windows were, that you couldn't see a single smudge on them. The lawn was mowed short and neat. The flower beds were a riot of color and heady fragrance. Olivia couldn't help but be drawn into this fairy-tale home, for she knew just looking at it that the adults that lived here were happy, healthy, and so very much in love with each other and their children.

Maybe that was why the woman that was standing on the front lawn looking toward the upper windows was so out of place.

"Well goddamn, isn't that something to see?" Sari chuckled, taking in the naked woman standing on the lawn, oblivious to the group's arrival.

"Only you would find humor in this situation, Sari, for Christ's sake," Olivia scolded.

"Come on, girl, how often do you turn a corner and come across a flesh-and-blood lawn ornament, designed after a Greek goddess?"

"It isn't Aphrodite standing there, and I doubt she even belongs here."

Olivia looked over her shoulder at her fellow coworkers and saw shock and concern on most of their faces. She also quickly noticed that John's face was so red that he might have a stroke right there if someone didn't DO something right that instant. On the other hand, Sari's face was full of humor and glee, highly amused by the entire situation. Shaking her head with the knowledge that not one of them was going to do anything, Olivia took charge of the situation.

"Stop gawking and give me your jacket, Dave. Now. And someone call 911," Olivia firmly stated. Shaking her head and reaching out a hand to take the jacket, she walked quickly but calmly over to the woman standing in the yard and draped the jacket over her shoulders. The woman did not move or even acknowledge the kind gesture, she just continued to stare at the home. Olivia asked the woman her name, though knowing that she would not get an answer. She just kept praying that no one was home to see what was transpiring on their perfectly manicured front lawn.

"Goddamnit," she mumbled, seeing the front door begin to open, watching a gentleman in dress attire walk out to address the group of people standing oddly in front of his home, the protectiveness coming off him in waves.

"Can I help you? Why is it that you are all standing on my lawn?" the gentleman questioned as his wife appeared beside him. She let out a little cry of shock and the husband turned to see what had frightened her. All eyes turned to the naked woman, who was now twitching and mumbling, standing on the front lawn, staring up at the windows, still not registering the other people around her, or the jacket that Olivia had attempted to cover her with.

She stood there completely naked, her body all curves and generous slopes, skin soft and unmarred by scars or tattoos, likely a very pretty woman when not so drugged up that she had no concept of reality. Her long blonde hair hung down her back, twigs and dirt adorning the strands like dirty accessories. One could tell by looking at her that she was new to the Ink scene. She hadn't lost her looks yet, but soon she would be covered in lesions and the skin would be pulled taut around her face from lack of nutrition. Constantly chasing the need for the next high, always and forever searching for the feeling of that first high, the one that started it all. She was someone's sister, friend, daughter, lover, but none of that mattered to her now. She didn't have a thought or care for any of that, or anything except for those upper windows for that matter.

Sending his wife back inside to keep the children away from the windows, the man approached the task force, who assured him that they had already contacted the authorities who were on their way. He moved forward in an aggressive manner, as though to assert his authority over the stranger standing in his yard. Olivia addressed him softly. "It won't do you any good. She hasn't responded to anything, even the touch of the jacket on her skin. Don't make matters worse. You don't know what she might be on or what may have happened to her before she ended up here."

Throwing her a death stare, he grumbled unhappily and moved to talk to John, their group leader, to demand answers as to who they all were.

"We are part of Clean Our Streets Task Force, or COST, a program that has been put together through a partnership between the National Environmental Directive (NED) and Regional Environmental Directive (RED) to clean up our streets, to bring safety back to neighborhoods, and to try to solve the seemingly never-ending drug epidemic that has plagued our state," John stated. "We are called in to determine if cities, villages, and towns qualify for assistance from the government." A look of interest and hope crossed the man's face as he explained to the group that he was on the city board and worked in finance.

"There seems to be a never-ending supply of Ink in our town. I remember when my family and I could walk the streets at any time of the day or night and feel safe. Now we can't even walk out of our front door without being assailed with this epidemic."

Nodding his head sympathetically, John reached up and patted the gentleman's shoulder, ever the bureaucrat. "We will do what we can for you and your town. We need to gather data from our surveys and run the numbers, but here is my card if you have any questions."

"What kind of data do you need? My office may be able to help."

"What agency do you work for?"

Puffing up his chest, the homeowner replied, "I work in City Hall. I'm on the mayor's council."

"Excellent. Anything related to Ink usage is helpful. Things like the number of arrests, hospitalizations, deaths, and rehabilitation cases. We also do a visual survey, which is what we are conducting currently."

The conversation between the men continued as Olivia felt nausea rising in her stomach. They acted as though this woman were not standing right there listening to every word. Olivia rolled her eyes as she watched Dave join in on the conversation, fitting right into that mold.

She looked at the woman, taking in her nakedness, her vulnerability, and her utter lack of realization that she was indeed naked and vulnerable. It didn't look as though she had been harmed in any way thankfully. She was just a sad sight, the poster child for the drug epidemic that continued to spread daily across the region. Olivia's heart went out to those that loved the person this woman had been, and still was, though they likely didn't know how to help her. So many of these situations occurred every single day with no positive outlook for tomorrow to be better. "Hold on to hope. Fight for those that you love. Don't let the drug take them," were words she often heard. As if it were that simple and easy.

Dave caught the strange look on Olivia's face and removed himself from the conversation. "Hey, are you okay?"

A frown spread across her face, and she replied, "It just reminds me of... Ugh, never mind. I think I can hear the sirens. Took them long enough!"

The sound finally pulled the woman from her trance and she looked around at all of the people gathered near her, though appearing not to really see them, and watched the police pull up at the front curb, the jacket falling to the ground and exposing her entire body to the world again. She began to make a tiny mewling sound, much like the scrawny kitten back at the grocery store. Olivia noticed urine running down the woman's legs, pooling on the ground and all over Dave's jacket. Olivia turned and her eyes met Sari's dark almond-shaped eyes, which were bathed in humor.

"I really don't know how you find humor in everything."

Sari laughed. "Girl, let me tell you, it is better to laugh than to cry. Besides, did you know that Dave just bought that jacket this past weekend? Look at his face!"

Looking absolutely disgusted, Dave said, "Guess that can just stay right there now. Olivia, you owe me a new jacket! It wasn't cheap you know."

Olivia surveyed the growing crowd. All the men that had had desire in their eyes towards the woman's nakedness were now all looking at her with condemnation and revulsion in their eyes.

Serves them right. We aren't here for the viewing pleasure of men.

As the police moved toward the woman, sudden fear blossomed in her eyes, and she turned to run, but in her drug-induced state she clearly didn't realize that her feet were caught up in the urine-soaked jacket, and she fell heavily to the ground. She scrambled to get up, crawling on her hands and knees to get away, merely giving the group that was watching a show of her nether regions and the piercing that resided down there. Then the police were upon her, cuffing her and pulling her roughly to her feet.

"Please, don't take me away. Please, I will do whatever you want, please. I promise to be good," begged the woman who was now standing unsteadily, being held by the officers so she couldn't harm herself or anybody else.

Everyone, every single person in that crowd, ignored her pleas, acting like she wasn't even there, not a human being restrained on a pristine lawn but a disease covered in flesh that no one wanted to catch.

Olivia came up beside her, asking, "What can I do to help you? Do you have family or friends that I can call for you?"

The woman frowned, her body swaying, lips full and almost seductive if they weren't so filthy, and said, "Someone like you could never understand. You're just one of those uptight bitches that look down on girls like me. Go fuck yourself."

"I understand far more than you realize. I was... engaged to a beautiful woman that got caught up in Ink and it destroyed us in ways that you cannot fathom." Feeling a sudden surge of anger, Olivia snapped. "You have no clue what this is doing to whoever may love you. Only worried about the drug... never what's really important in life. You and those like you can be so selfish!"

A young officer reached out to Olivia, drawing her away. "Don't concern yourself with Miss Sabrina here. She might be new to the scene, but we have already had three calls involving her in the past week."

Olivia tried to gain control of her emotions as she listened to the officer explain that this was a regular occurrence. How many more situations like this would there be before Sabrina ended up in the morgue or raped and murdered by some criminal wandering the streets at night just like her? This wasn't a huge city, but it certainly had dark places and was developing a dark reputation for the crimes that were being committed here daily. Her hometown was one of the top twenty in the region for crimes, especially related to drugs, and she felt like it was her job to set things right again, but how?

The question remained with her as the ambulance came and took Sabrina away, allowing the family to go back to their everyday life and the task force to continue with their job, as though nothing had happened. Olivia wanted to scream at the top of her lungs, her frustration with this society at its final measure. Dave must have sensed her growing frustration because he walked up to her and put his arm around her, lightly caressing her shoulder.

He leaned in gently, resting his forehead against hers. "It's going to be alright, Olivia. They are going to help get her cleaned up and call her family. She will be off the streets at least for today."

Olivia pulled away with her head high, determination back in place within her mind.

"It's just so much more than that, Dave, and no I don't really want to talk about it, but thanks for being a friend."

"Liv, come on, I don't know why you won't let me get close and help you. You always keep me at arm's length."

"What are you talking about, Dave? We're good friends. At least I thought we were."

A huge sigh erupted out of Dave. "We should get back to work, I guess. Which area is next on the list?"

Olivia glanced over her shoulder, eyebrow arched high. "We need to meet the others at the diner downtown to discuss our assessments."

The small group headed downtown, making their way down the tree-lined streets, looking at the subtle signs of the world falling apart at its seams. The strange incident with the naked woman clearly played back in each of their minds, on repeat, each of them wondering what possible solution there could be to keep everyone safe and reasonably happy. Olivia, like the others, was thinking of things that made her happy and how those things could be used to ensure happiness and safety for everyone.

But then her mind slipped back a couple years, to a time when she felt happy, on the beach, sun warming her skin, looking at the hand that she held in hers, thinking of what those hands could do to her, feeling passion rushing through her body...

"Oh my god! That's it! I know what to do now!" Olivia exclaimed loudly, startling Dave, John, and her other two coworkers.

2

The diner was cozy and warm, scents filling the air with their tantalizing aromas. It was just enough to make the mouth water and trigger the desire to sample the many offerings on the menu. A quiet buzz filled the air as people went about their conversations with each other while silverware softly pinged against dishes. Occasionally laughter would erupt from a table, drawing brief glances, pulling people out of their own worlds to remind them that they were not alone here.

John looked over his crew, his gaze falling to rest on Olivia. "What was the epiphany that came to you earlier? You seemed quite sure that you knew what could be done to help the Ink epidemic."

"Okay, hear me out. Don't judge until you hear the entire plan. Deal?"

Nods and assurances moved through the group as they patiently waited for her to begin.

She took a deep breath and began. "The homeowners and other citizens want to be able to have safe and clean cities, towns, and such. The Ink addicts want to be able to live their lives as they see fit as well, right? So, what if we were able to provide that for both parties?"

Dave piped up, voicing what they were all thinking. "How is that even possible, Olivia? It's not like you can make Ink safer to use or addicts less of a problem."

"See, that's part of the actual problem with society. Those that are not addicts feel as though they can place their expectations on those that are addicts. They want them to conform to their ways instead of being able to live as they choose. My idea can offer both parties what they want if I can get the support for it."

"I'm interested," Sari said quietly.

"An island. We create a community for addicts on an island so that they can live their lives as they see fit while not being a so-called nuisance for the general public. The government has many islands off the coast that they own. It would just be a matter of building the community and getting people there."

After a brief silence, they all started asking questions at once, giving their opinions, and outright questioning the possibility of something like that being accepted. Olivia sat patiently waiting for the group to settle down before trying to continue.

"I can't answer you all at once so how about you each get one question. I don't have it worked out perfectly in my mind yet, but the rough draft is there."

As the group leader, John asked first. "Even if you can convince the government, how do you propose to get the general public to agree to such a thing?"

"I am sure that whoever ends up running the operation can hold press conferences and build an educational outreach program that will inform people of what the goal of the island is."

Dave piped up next. "What about sex?"

"I'm not even sure what you mean by that question, Dave. Seriously, is that all that you think about?"

"No, like what about women getting pregnant and all that stuff? Diseases, sickness, you know, the bad stuff that comes with sex sometimes."

"Oh okay. My idea would be to have a health center on the island. It would be a full community, like a small village, with all the perks of life on the mainland."

Eyebrow raised, Sari asked, "Where will you get funding for your addict village, Liv? It sounds great in theory but all of that will require a lot of money. If you are going to be asking the government to fund it then what that really means is tax dollars. I'm not so sure that the people of our nation will be supportive of that. What you are suggesting is basically taxpayer money buying drugs for addicts just so that they can feel safe and have clean streets. Why should we have to pay for their habits?"

"That will be the difficult part for sure, but I really think that it's worth a shot. Currently we are spending immense amounts of money on our prison system, extra officers on the streets, and so many rehabilitation programs. If we look at the numbers, do some cost accounting, we could determine what the difference is and which side it favors. There isn't any reason why we shouldn't try something new. It's obvious that the system as is doesn't work."

Leaning back, arms crossed over her chest, Sari asserted, "Sure, but why would the government give up any of its budget for a druggie's paradise, Liv?"

Dave jumped in. "Right! Why should taxpayers have to worry about funding these people's habits? I know I don't want to have my money taken and given away to some drug addict so they can be free to OD on some island."

Mouth turning down at the corners, chin held high, Olivia responded, "It's a great idea. That money is already being spent in ways that do nothing to fix the problem of cleaning up the cities. DO any of you even know how your tax dollars are being spent currently?"

The faces around the table grew red, and their heads bowed down or turned to look out the windows. Olivia spoke again, shaking her head. "That's what I thought."

"Listen, we aren't saying the idea is trash, we just don't see the government supporting it. That's all, Liv. Don't be mad, 'kay? Let's table it for now and come back to it another time," suggested Sari.

Murmurs of agreement were voiced as the conversation began to drift to more mundane things. Tuning everyone out, Olivia was brought to a place of nostalgia by the gentle hustle and bustle of the diner as she remembered eating here occasionally with her parents and then later in life with friends after a night out on the town. For a moment, the happiness faded as she also remembered bringing Aria here to meet her parents before they moved out of the area.

That had been an exciting but nerve-wracking day for both Olivia and Aria. Olivia had an apartment in town at the time, so it seemed best to meet on neutral ground. She had been worried that they wouldn't accept that she had chosen to be with a woman instead of a man. Olivia knew that her parents had high hopes of being grandparents even though she had already explained that she didn't really want to bring children into this world as it was.

Olivia had rummaged through the closet looking for the perfect outfit before catching Aria's eye, who was sitting on the bed in nothing but lace panties. Desire surged through Olivia as Aria ran her hands down under that tiny piece of lace, slowly opening her legs so Olivia could watch her pleasure herself. Aria's head fell back with a moan as she slid her fingers deep inside herself. Olivia moved to the bedside, wet and ready to fall under Aria's spell...

"Hello! Earth to Olivia. Where did you go?" Sari questioned, pulling Olivia back to the present.

Olivia looked down at the table, hoping to hide the deep scarlet of embarrassment showing on her face. Shaking her head clear, she looked up just as the waitress arrived with their food. The scent tantalized and distracted them from questioning Olivia's daydreaming.

As they ate, Olivia contemplated the day and all that had happened. She recognized the martyr in herself, always wanting to fix and save everyone. She needed to do something. Something that could have a positive impact on any life.

Her train of thought was interrupted by Dave asking, "Hey do you guys want to grab a drink after we finish up here?"

She thought about it for a moment and replied, "No thanks. I have to see if I can save a life before heading back home," dismissing her friends' quizzical glances to each other as she rose and walked out of the diner alone.

3

Bright sunlight shone through the sheer curtains that covered the large bay window on the east side of the room, warming the bedcovers and pulling a sleepy murmur from Olivia's mouth. She snuggled down further into the soft blankets, enjoying the silky feel on her skin, caressing her body like a lover, holding her safe and warm just a few minutes longer. It was Saturday. No need to get up too early. A lovely day to lounge around the house, have some coffee while reading the paper, maybe workout a little later, shower, and relax for the rest of the day. *One of the best things about living alone was not having to work around anybody else's schedule,* she thought sleepily. Although it did get lonely sometimes. The intrusive thought slipped in, but she swatted it away like a gnat. Needless thoughts had no place in her warm, cozy bed.

Mrrrow.

Startled, Olivia sat straight up in bed, covers falling from her naked body, looking for the source of that sound, eyes finally landing on the black malnourished kitten.

"Ah, pretty baby! I forgot about you. I guess it's time to get up and feed you, huh?"

She thought back to the previous evening, the meeting just finishing up, Sari and Dave asking her if she wanted to go out for a drink, and her declining and going to find this little black furball instead. She had been determined to help someone or something from her hometown that day. The kitten, whom she had named Max, was surprisingly easy to catch, almost like he knew that she was there to save him.

She glanced over at the nightstand and saw her laptop still open. The blinking cursor on the typewritten page beckoning her to check her email. Emboldened by saving the kitten, she had come home and turned the idea into a proposal and sent it out before she could chicken out.

There was no way the RED had seen the email yet.

In an attempt to shake off the worry she scooped the kitten up, holding him against her bare skin, and walked into the kitchen to find the food she had grabbed at the late-night convenience store on her way home. She puttered around the kitchen, waiting for her coffee to brew while the kitten ate hungrily, only pausing to watch her move from one side of the kitchen island to the other. Olivia laughed out loud at Max when he jumped, startled by the coffeepot hissing and spitting, filling the air with its delicious aroma. She was reaching for a coffee mug when a sudden loud knock on her front door made her jump, her coffee mug thankfully landing on the counter. She looked at Max, who was almost smirking, as if to say, *serves you right for laughing at me.*

Better not be a solicitor, she grumbled as she headed for the bedroom to grab her robe, short, pink, and so soft that it tickled her body as she walked. Peeking through the peephole, she sighed, unlocking the door. "What brings you by so early, Sari? I would think that you'd still be in bed after going out last night."

"We didn't go out since you bailed; apparently, I'm not a good enough time for our dear friend Dave, or maybe I'm too much fun for him to handle all on his own! Haha." Leaning in to kiss Olivia on the cheek, Sari glanced at the kitchen doorway, where two little green eyes stared back.

"Seriously? Is this why you took off so quickly last night after the meeting? I should have known you would have to try to save something! Always the crusader."

"I couldn't just leave him there. He would have died sooner or later, and you know it." Laughing quietly, Olivia added, "Sari meet Max, the new love of my life."

"Well, isn't he just the scrawniest thing?" Sari reached out to pet the tiny ball of fluff. "At least he doesn't smell bad. How did you get him cleaned up so well?"

"Surprisingly, he didn't seem to mind when I gave him a Dawn dish-soap bath. That's what it said to do when I googled it."

"He is going to be a cat of luxury now! Pampered and spoiled," laughed Sari. "Hey, maybe I could be your kitty too! Then you could pamper and spoil me."

"Sari, as much as I love you, I'm not sure that I could afford you or your tastes."

"Aww, come on, Liv, Max and I match. You know you can't resist a dark-skinned beauty." Winking lavishly with a deep and infectious laugh, Sari pulled Olivia over into an embrace. "Come on, honey, get your sassy ass dressed and let's go out for some shopping therapy and lunch. We need it after yesterday."

"I was planning on staying in and having a chill day at home."

She leaned a hip on the counter, patiently waiting as Sari moved to the coffee maker and poured a cup of coffee and flavored it with creamer. Olivia, her hair long and dark, looking silky even though it was still unbrushed, moved to make her own cup of black coffee. Looking up, her deep blue eyes met Sari's dark eyes. Seeing the obvious appreciation in them, Olivia blushed deeply, her chest becoming flushed and hot.

Sari busted out in delightful laughter. "You know it's not like that, Liv. No need to get all hot and bothered. Haha. Go get dressed; we're going to get some takeout before hibernating here all day." Becoming a bit more serious, as serious as Sari possibly could be, she said, "I know yesterday hit hard. I know what it brought you back to. I'm not leaving you to sulk through the day alone, babe."

"I'm fine, seriously! You don't need to babysit me, Sari. I'm not a lost little girl."

The look of immovable determination on her friend's face made Olivia sigh deeply. "Fine, I'll go get dressed, but I get to choose the food AND the movie!"

She could hear Sari talking softly to Max as she made her way back to her bedroom. So much for a day of relaxation and doing nothing. Sari was a good friend though, always had been, ever since they interned together at the regional office building just out of university. The two of them were like night and day in almost every way, but it worked well for them. It was nice to have someone that knew when you shouldn't be alone, someone to keep you honest and grounded.

Occasionally, there was a sexual pull, but it was never anything serious, and neither of them had ever acted on it. It was unlikely that they ever would. Sari was drop-dead gorgeous, and she knew it. That confidence shone everywhere they went. She never had to go home alone from a night out, unless that was the chosen course of action. Sari also had serious commitment issues; well maybe not issues, just an immense lack of desire to settle down with one person at any time in the near future.

Olivia tossed her bathrobe on the bed in a pink heap and caught sight of herself in the full-length closet mirrors. She looked over her naked body trying to see what Sari, or even Dave, saw when they looked at her with desire in their eyes. She had nice hair, long, dark, and wavy, and eyes that could be called a startling bright blue. She made sure to keep herself in shape, so her figure was decent, she supposed. She spun around, slowly taking it in, her firm round behind, flat stomach, and C-cup breasts tipped with dark brown areolas. I'm a solid above average, I guess. I suppose I can see what they find intriguing.

With her eyes closed, she thought back to those hands again, the ones that were always able to create a fire within, starting in the belly and spreading slow and steady, the heat growing and building, her own hands softly moving along her abdomen.

"FUCK," she snarled out loud, her hands leaving her body and fisting at her sides. Yesterday had really pushed her two steps back to where she had been in the whole healing process. She angrily snagged shorts and a T-shirt from her closet and threw them on.

Sari's eyebrows raised as Olivia entered the room in a much different mood than when she had left it. "You alright, Liv? You look madder than a wet hen… not that I've ever seen a wet hen. Hahaha."

"Just dandy; let's get this show on the road." Snatching the keys from the counter and moving toward the front door, she said, "I'm driving."

"Wait, what? My car? Are you sure you are in the right frame of mind to drive my car, babe?"

Olivia shot her a quick look and flashed a smile. "Since when are you chicken?"

"You did not call me that! Just remember, beautiful, you break it, you buy it."

Sliding into the smooth black leather seats of the bright red 1969 Chevy Camaro, Olivia turned the key in the ignition, adrenaline rushing through her veins as the engine growled to life. The car rumbled and vibrated with all the waiting horsepower under the hood, ready to be unleashed. Slipping her hairband off her wrist, she deftly swept her long dark hair up into a messy bun and put on her designer sunglasses to shade her eyes. Remembering at the last minute to buckle up, she glanced sideways at Sari and let loose a playful giggle. "Ready to rock?"

"Oh honey, I was born ready. The real question here is, can you handle all this power underneath you?" Sari asked suggestively, sitting back stretched out in the passenger seat, all confidence and sex appeal on that hot black leather.

Letting loose a wild laugh and dropping the shifter down into drive, Olivia peeled away from her house and the dark memories that she'd conjured there only a short time ago. Clouds of smoke rose from the street as the tires squealed, the air heavy with the smell of burning rubber, the engine coming to life, the release fast and hard, surging forward, catching her by surprise with the sheer power of the bored-out engine. With everything forgotten for the moment, she drove fast and furiously, rounding corners with the squeal of tires, speeding up streets meant for slow cruising, driving all thoughts from her mind, living and breathing speed and fresh air, power and precision. Breathless and exhilarated, Olivia found the adrenaline rush clearing her mind.

When they finally came to a T in the road, Sari asked, "Well, where are we going, babe, because the city is about five miles in the other direction."

"I want the coast, the water, the curves, the sea air. It's only a little farther. Can we?"

"What about your pretty little kitty Max?"

"I'm sure he will be fine. He has food, water, and a clean litter box." With her big bright blue eyes pleading, Olivia asked, "Can we, please?"

"I'm a sucker for those baby blues; we can go wherever you want, Liv. You've got me wrapped around that little finger of yours, you know."

"Yes! You are the best!"

"I may have heard that a time or two, though usually from someone straddling me."

"You are incorrigible," Olivia laughed, making a left onto the county road, speeding toward the coastal highway and all its dangerous curves and scenic views.

With music blasting, the windows down, and them singing along with the radio, both were lost in the moment. The trees and grass along the road swept by, mostly unseen, a blur in their vision. Nothing else mattered except the road. They reached the coastal highway quickly and cruised along the cliff, slower now, taking in the wide view of the big blue ocean. Though the anger that Olivia had felt earlier had dissipated, sadness clung to her like an unseen spiderweb, wrapping its silky and sticky threads around her heart.

Pulling over at a scenic viewpoint, they watched waves breaking over each other in a race to get to shore, only to hurry back out into the open water, the constant ebb and flow of the tide a cycle repeating itself for eternity. It was a bit cathartic for her as she equated it with the emotions that came and went, her heart hurting for the life she should have.

"Let's live on the beach, Sari, enjoy the simple life, you know?" Olivia said wistfully, looking out at the ocean.

"It's a thought to consider. Not sure I could settle in one place though, ya know?"

"The beach has always been my place, my go-to when things aren't right or even when things are." Olivia sighed deeply. "I always feel at least content when I'm there."

Hearing the longing in her voice, Sari commented, "It's easy to imagine all is right in the world when you are staring at clear blue skies, the sun warming your body, listening to the ocean waves lapping at the shore, and drinking in that salty sea air." Glancing at Olivia sideways, she said, "But that doesn't last forever. There are going to be stormy skies too. You've got to come back to reality sometime, Liv."

Avoiding the possibility of a serious conversation, Olivia exclaimed, "Hey, there is a little food truck right off the highway before the beach entrance, about a mile down! Let's go grab a bite. I'm starving!"

"You are always starving, Livi! Haha. Let's go. They better have chili dogs. The messier the better!"

The smell of grilled hot dogs, nacho cheese, warm pretzels, and something super sweet drifted through the windows of the Camaro before they had even parked. So enticing were the scents that neither of them noticed the group of people watching them pull into the parking lot, eyeing the car appreciatively. When Olivia finally realized the number of people staring at her, she began to blush deeply, not liking so much attention all at once. Sari continued to lounge comfortably in the passenger seat, loving the attention, completely used to being fawned over for both the car and being drop-dead gorgeous.

"I don't know how you can stand being looked at like this, like you and your car are pieces of meat or possessions to acquire," a bright-red-faced Olivia replied.

"Neither I nor my car can be acquired as a possession. Both belong only to me, Liv. That's how I like it, and I don't see that changing any-time soon, with very few exceptions."

Sliding out of the car, hair ravaged from the wind coming in through the open windows, and feeling incredibly self-conscious, Olivia attempted to stride confidently to the throng of people waiting in line for the food truck with Sari swaggering alongside, cool as a cucumber, winking at the ones staring. Olivia found herself scanning the ground for used needles as she walked, frowning when she realized what she was doing. It follows me everywhere I go. I can't ever seem to let it go and just have a good time. Ugh!

Delicious scents drifted over to them from the truck, pulling her from her anxiety, making them soon forget everything but their stom-achs growling hungrily.

"I swear I could eat a horse. It smells so good. Thanks for suggesting I get out of the house, Sari."

"My pleasure. I've been wanting to get down here anyway. I haven't been down here since that last woman that I was bedding threatened to make a scene the next time she saw me. She knew I came down here at least once a week, but I hear she has moved on finally. They do get easily addicted to my charms!"

"She was a bit high-strung, even for you, but didn't you tell her that you had no intention of committing right from the start?"

"I always do. I spell it out in black and white from the very first moment, but they always think that they can change my mind. I guess that's what I get for being so amazing. I don't blame her for wanting to try to lock me down."

"You are so full of yourself, good lord!"

"Nah babe, I'm just honest to a fault. If you ever want to find out just how good I am in bed, you just let me know. Then you will know firsthand just how truthful I am."

"Ha! Let's get our food and go sit in the sun for a while," Olivia said, shaking her head, laughing quietly. Olivia loved Sari for so many reasons, but honesty was definitely one of the big reasons there was such trust between them. If only everyone were that honest with themselves and each other, maybe my life would be different now, she thought to herself.

Sitting at the picnic table with the sun warming their skin, they ate contentedly, going on and on about how good the food was and making a deal to come down there at least every other week to try something new together. Olivia laughed at herself, nacho cheese and chili all over her fingers, and probably her face, but it was a feeling of childlike delight. She licked the food from her fingers before grabbing a napkin and cleaning up the rest of her mess. If only life could be this easy all the time, but that's impossible. It was then that she noticed a woman around five feet away, golden skin and lush brown hair much like Aria's, flirting with a man that had just been sitting with another woman.

Dark thoughts took her once again, transporting her to another beach, a feeling of inadequacy coming over her, watching what was said to be harmless flirting taking place. Harmless. Ha. Was that when the tides had changed? That fleeting moment of supposed harmless flirtation? Shaking her head to rid herself of the thought, Olivia came back to reality to feel a hand lying on her thigh simply for comfort. There was a look in Sari's eyes that seemed to be saying, I know where you were, and I am here for you.

"Let's head back to the house, grab a movie on the way, and maybe some wine," Olivia suggested.

"Are you sure you want to be drinking tonight, darling? Your head has been wandering around some tender subjects the past couple of days. I don't want you to do anything you might regret, Liv."

"Wine or whisky, Sari, your call."

"Alright, alright. Wine and a horror movie. Don't worry, babe, I will keep you safe from the monsters under your bed." Sari lavishly winked and reached for the keys. "I'm driving this time."

The car engine started with a roar and with music blasting they peeled out of the parking lot, making people stop and stare with envious looks. Olivia sat back, closed her eyes, and attempted to relax for once. She listened to the music, letting it fill her, feeling the beat and vibration of the music inside. As the song ended, the radio personality came on, announcing breaking news.

"Suspects from an alleged home robbery are being sought after one of them was left behind, apparently overdosing on what was believed to be the drug Ink. Officers administered a lifesaving drug in an attempt to revive the suspect, but there are no further details on their condition. No one in the home was harmed in the break-in. A mother and her child were in the residence when the alleged robbery occurred. They hid in a bedroom closet and called emergency services. The suspects are on the loose and considered to be armed and dangerous. If anyone has any information, please contact the regional police immediately and do not approach the suspects."

With her mouth turned down at the corners, fear and frustration collided within Olivia. "This is exactly what my idea could keep from happening," Olivia sighed.

"Have you typed up the proposal yet?" Sari asked quietly.

"Yes, I finished it last night after I got home and emailed it to the Regional Environmental Directive."

"You're such an overachiever, Liv." Taking her hand and squeezing it lightly, Sari said, "You will make it happen. If anyone can do it, babe, it's you."

"I really hope they will take it seriously. I think it could work out for everyone's benefit," Olivia said, shrugging doubtfully. "I looked into some of the costs and obstacles that could be presented as an issue. The government already owns a chain of islands that isn't being used for anything. It used to be a military base and has some usable structures. I also ran some numbers. It wouldn't raise taxes much at all to implement this project."

"That is amazing, Liv, and I know that you're excited, but enough shoptalk. Let's go get the scariest movie that we can find, one that will have you jumping into my lap and wrapping those sexy arms around me."

The laughter and sarcasm continued all the way into the night, but in the back of Olivia's mind, she worried. Was her idea going to be taken seriously and would it really work like she had drawn out?

4

The alarm buzzed even before Max could make his way onto the bed to demand breakfast. Olivia blinked herself awake while silencing the alarm. She pulled him to her chest to snuggle as he made his way onto the bed. His warmth and purring were so comforting that she couldn't understand why she hadn't gotten a cat before this. He offered such uncomplicated love and affection. It was so much simpler than the affection and love between humans. Boy, did they really fuck all of that up; conditions on everything, never being happy or appreciating what they had, and wanting too much. Although in her previous situation, she didn't think that she had asked for too much. She had been happy with the simple life.

She stopped herself before the thoughts went too far. That was enough of that tragic train of thought. It was time to get ready for work.

Today was an office day where the team would touch base and complete data entry on all the assessments that had been completed over the last two weeks. She loved working for COST, really, but being back in her hometown, along with the drugged-woman situation, had just dragged her into her past. She needed to focus on the future. She had a plan if only the directors would give her a chance to show them how and why it was such a great idea.

She hopped out of bed and went down the hall to the kitchen to start coffee and feed Max before jumping in the shower. The kitten ran happily down the hallway in front of her. Food poured and coffee brewed. Olivia got in the shower, singing silly songs about love, the sunshine, and flowers all around. She could hear her phone ringing, but she continued to get ready for work. She slathered her body with cocoa butter, her skin smelling like a mix of marshmallows and chocolate.

The shining sun was warm and bright coming through the windows. She reveled in the feeling of it warming her naked skin, soothing and sensual in its own way. Taking a large swig of coffee, she picked up her phone and saw that she had a few missed calls: three messages from Sari and one from Dave. She opened Sari's first, which simply said check your email in all capital letters. She scrolled through her emails quickly and almost choked when she saw one from the RED.

Good morning Miss Titos. After reviewing your proposal we have some further questions. Please contact this office at your earliest convenience so that we may set an appointment for you to come in and discuss this matter.

Holy shit, they were really looking into her idea! Still in shock, she sat on the edge of her bed, trying to figure out what to do next. She checked the text from Dave and saw that it basically said the same thing that Sari's had, but with a different tone. He was probably upset that she hadn't contacted him at all this weekend. Ugh, men.

Walking into the common area an hour later, she was not surprised to see everyone there waiting for her, anxiety flooding through her before she could even walk into her office. The small table sat in the center of the beige-colored room, everyone eyeing her with anticipation. You could smell the lingering scent of toasted bagel hanging in the air. Suddenly there was a cascade of sound as they asked questions all at once, the excitement palpable in the room. This was a big deal to the entire team, especially if they went ahead with her idea and asked her to oversee the project, though that was unlikely. The RED usually had a handpicked team for the major jobs, ready and waiting to take on the next big idea.

Dave slung his arm around her as soon as she was close enough and breathed in deeply. "God, you smell good, Liv."

"Thanks. I think."

"Why are you acting like a dog, coming all up on her, sniffing and shit, dude?" Sari questioned. "No wonder you don't have a girl."

Dave glowered at Sari, but moved a respectable distance away from Olivia, who silently thanked Sari with her eyes.

"There's my rock star," boomed John. "I knew you were the brain of this dysfunctional group, Olivia. I am so proud of you. Just imagine where you can take us and COST!"

"Thank you, sir. I just want to make a difference. I want everyone to be able to live their best life and be happy. That looks different for all of us I suppose. So, hopefully this can benefit everyone."

Looking around the room, she promised, "I will let everyone know if they reach out to me directly, no worries, you guys."

Escaping to her cubicle, Olivia looked around at the small office that was staffed by good people, most of whom were her friends. She would certainly choose to work with them on this project if she got the go-ahead to lead, but first she had to see if the directors were really willing to put it out there to the public.

The gray walls, the darker gray carpet, the big floor-to-ceiling windows, the gentle hum of people working and talking... This was her place to make a difference in the world. Sitting at her desk, she thought of how different her life would have been if she hadn't been through such a trying time two short years ago.

Being engaged to an addict was not something that she had ever considered for her life. Not that Aria had started out that way, but her line of work took her to some rough places. Being an award-winning journalist came with its perks, but it also had its dark side.

That time she had gotten too caught up in the fray, and it had destroyed the Aria she had been, as well as her career and their relationship. Ink was a messy drug that ruined so many people's lives. On the other hand, doing drugs was a choice that was made, and if people wanted to live their lives that way, who was Olivia to say otherwise?

When life had been about to swallow her up, Sari swooped in as always to drag her to safety, suggesting she come to work here at the agency, giving her a glowing recommendation. She was hired on the spot, of course. She ended up loving the work most of the time and became incredibly good at it.

It was almost as though the thought of the past was enough to beckon her friend, because as Olivia looked up, there was Sari standing in front of her.

"Alright, I know you're keeping something a secret. I can tell by the look on your face, and because you didn't slap Dave away when he was up in your shit. Spill it, Liv."

Trying to avoid the subject, Olivia looked away from Sari's intense dark eyes, knowing that she wouldn't be able to lie, not to Sari. "Max is already putting on some weight, and his coat is getting silkier, I think. I can't wait to see how he grows now that he has a chance."

"That's great, Liv. I'm sure he hasn't changed much since I was there most of the night Saturday. He sat in my lap and fell asleep during the scariest movie ever. You know, the lap that you kept almost jumping into."

"Sari, that movie was terrifying! I had nightmares from it!"

"I offered to stay the night, keep you safe while you slept, which is beyond valiant in my opinion. Now stop hedging. Spill it."

"Fine, fine. The RED wasn't the only agency that I sent my proposal to. I sent it to the National Environmental Directive, NED, as well."

"What?" Dave exploded as he was creeping by, causing both of them to jump out of their skins. "You did what?"

"Goddamnit, Dave! Why are you always lurking around listening to everyone's conversations?"

"Listen Sari, I happen to work here too, and my desk is only two cubes down. Besides, you guys were talking so loudly, I'm surprised the entire office didn't hear what you said."

"Both of you relax. For crying out loud, what is this pissing contest between the two of you lately?"

"We are both madly in love with you and want to whisk you away," Sari drawled slowly. "Isn't that right, Dave?"

Sputtering, Dave growled, "God, Sari, you are fucking obnoxious!"

Olivia flushed, turning a bright apple-red, her irritation showing clearly on her face, "What the hell, guys? Why does everything have to be about sex? I don't even care about that anymore. I just want to do my job and help people out. Can we just focus on that? Please!"

"You're right, darling. We are both sorry."

"Yeah, yeah. But what about the NED? Have you heard anything from them?" Dave questioned.

"No, I haven't heard anything. It's national. They might not even acknowledge it. You know how it is with them, always saying they have a plan or want to help, but then it all falls to the RED."

"Maybe this time it will be different, Liv. Your plan is brilliant!"

"Thanks Dave. I hope they take a look at it, and at least consider it."

Olivia swiveled around and returned to her computer, listening to her coworkers walk away while conversing quietly. She didn't understand why they acted like rivals when in fact they all got along so well. People were so confusing sometimes, what with all of the grey areas of the human condition to traverse. Thankfully, her work was cut-and-dry, the right side of the line and the wrong side. She always stayed on the right side; the wrong side was far too much work.

Olivia began to shuffle through assessments, statistics, and ratios of the cities she had been to over the previous week, the information consuming her mind. She focused on the job at hand, plugging numbers into the system, the program deciding if the cities qualified for assistance from the state or if they would be denied. As bad as she felt about having to deny some towns, she understood that there was only so much funding to go around, and the worst cases needed to be helped first. In spite of the naked-woman incident, she knew that her hometown would not qualify for assistance through this program, even though it could really use it. In another five years, it would be likely to qualify, but unfortunately, right at that moment, there were not enough break-ins, deaths, murders, or other circumstances to prompt action on the task force's agency's part.

At least she had been able to save Max, her baby panther, as she liked to call him. Every woman should own a baby black panther, she thought laughingly to herself, continuing to trudge through all the paperwork on her desk and sifting through emails.

The day passed and there was still no word about her proposal from either the RED or NED. Sari and Dave approached Olivia with the question written on both of their faces. She spoke before they had the chance to ask her about it. "No, I haven't heard anything, guys. I will tell you if I do, alright?"

"Let's go grab a drink and some wings for dinner down at the bar, okay?" Dave suggested, in a clear attempt to reduce the tension that Olivia was feeling.

"Yeah Liv, let's do that," Sari agreed. "It's been a while since we've all hung out just for fun. All work and no play makes for a dull life. And I am anything but dull as you both know."

"Only if we go to the place that has the chicken wings that I like. You know, the really crispy ones! That bartender likes Dave anyway. Maybe he can get her number this time. She always gives us extra goodies." Olivia laughed. "Just let me finish these documents up and I will meet you guys there. It's easier to take separate cars."

Nodding in agreement, Dave and Sari went their separate ways, calling out goodbyes to the rest of the team in the office.

Olivia found the drive downtown to the local pub short and uneventful, but finding parking was a little tricky. It seemed like everyone was going out for happy-hour drinks tonight. She was sure that her coworkers would already be there, bellies up to the bar, flirting mercilessly with the ladies. She also knew that her order of wings and her favorite drink would be waiting for her when she walked in because they always made sure to look out for each other.

Walking through the door, she encountered a dimly lit hallway. The walls were a warm lacquered wood, neon signs flashing all around, and the scent of buffalo chicken wings in the air made her mouth water. The music was loud, but not too loud, just enough so that you had to lean in to hear someone talking to you. It made for an intimate experience, if you were into that sort of thing, which Olivia was not at this point in her life. No way. She was just here to hang out with her friends and eat some of the best chicken wings in town, have a couple drinks, and go home to Max.

She had to admit the atmosphere was a bit intoxicating though. It almost made her want to find a dark corner and lean in close to listen to someone speak, their fingers brushing the hair away from her face, their soft breath on her neck, her pulse beginning to race, and their eyes locking before an intense, passionate kiss. I really need to stop reading those romance novels or something, Olivia thought to herself as she caught sight of Dave at the bar. She hopped up onto the stool that she knew was being saved for her. "Is Sari here yet?"

"Yeah, just using the restroom, I think. We ordered your wings; they should be up soon."

"You guys are the best, you know. I couldn't ask for better friends. Oh, by the way, here is a surprise for you. I was going to give it to you earlier, but I forgot it in the trunk of my car."

Taking the bag and reaching inside, Dave began to chuckle as he threw the black leather jacket around his broad shoulders "Aw, Liv, you really didn't have to buy me a new jacket. It's really nice though. The leather is smooth as butter. I love it."

"I did have to. It's my fault that yours got pissed on, and it was on sale, so no big deal, really."

Chicken wings were placed in front of her by the pretty little brunette bartender that had a thing for Dave. "Thanks doll, they look delicious!" The scent was making Olivia's mouth water as she reached in and grabbed one. She sank her teeth into the wing and moaned with delight. The spiciness of the buffalo sauce had just enough kick to tantalize her taste buds, topped with the perfect crispy texture. "These are the best wings in the entire world, I swear!"

Sari laughed at her while moving up to the bar and taking hold of a beer, drinking half of it in one swallow.

"I don't know how you do that, Sari. I would throw up."

Not about to be outdone, Dave lifted his beer. "You do it like this," he said, tipping the bottle back and chugging almost the entire thing.

The brunette shimmied up, batting her eyelashes at Dave. "You need another drink, sugar?"

"Sure, I'll have another. Thanks."

Smiling sweetly, she said suggestively, "Anything for you," before she left to get him his drink.

Busting out laughing, Sari reached for another drink. "Hey Dave, maybe you should get her number this time."

"I'm not that great with women, Sari. I'm not you."

"Oh, touché, my friend. Though I will say , all you have to do is slip her your number or ask for hers. It's easy. I promise."

"You can do it, Dave," Olivia encouraged as she watched from the sidelines, devouring her chicken wings, happy that Sari was trying to help Dave out with his insecurities. She sipped on her whiskey, looking at her two friends and letting out a joyous laugh. "I really love you guys. You always make me laugh, even if I'm in a bad mood."

Bowing dramatically, both Sari and Dave simultaneously murmured, "At your service, madam."

Laughter erupted from the group, more drinks were served, and more chicken wings were consumed.

The group moved to the dance floor, bringing along a few others from the bar, letting loose a little after a busy Monday at work. Time passed and the crowd began to thin out, people heading home for dinner, the atmosphere shifting to the night crowd. Olivia looked at her watch and jolted. "I have to get home to Max!"

Startled, Dave said, "Who the hell is Max and why haven't I heard of him before now?"

"Oh," Sari said, "like you have some sort of right to know everything that goes on in her life, Dave. Nah, she is her own woman, and she doesn't answer to you, man. Or me for that matter, but at least I know about Max. He is a pretty awesome fella."

"Do you really need to rub that in his face, Sari? Come on now. However, Dave, I don't appreciate you speaking to me like that. I don't answer to anyone. That's the joy of being single, my friend."

"Listen, I'm sorry. I was just surprised, that's all," Dave spoke meekly.

"Max is my kitten. Do you remember the skinny black kitten in the last town we assessed? The one that was wandering around in front of the grocery store. I went back and rescued him. That's why I didn't go out for a drink with you guys after work that night."

Sari laughed hysterically as Dave's face turned a deep shade of red. "You got all pissed over a cat, man!"

"Don't pick on him so bad, Sari, geez. I've got to head out. See you tomorrow at the office."

Olivia walked out of the bar, and was heading to the car when her phone went off. She waited until she slid into her silver BMW before looking to see who it was. Shock waves rolled through her when she saw that she had multiple emails, one from the RED stating that they needed to hear from her immediately upon arrival at work the next morning for an interview concerning the project, and another from the NED reaching out, wanting to set up a meeting with her as well.

"Holy shit, they all read my project plan. Oh my god, this could really be happening!"

5

Olivia had planned to get to the office early and talk to her team before she had to meet with the RED. She hadn't told any of them about the emails she had received the night before because she was still processing it and wanted to keep it close to the vest for a bit. This would be such a huge opportunity if she didn't mess it up by dropping the ball somehow, and there were so many ways to do just that. She hadn't slept much the previous night, even with Max curled up warm and purring beside her. Her mind had run through every possibility, every question they might ask, every way she could think of that she might screw this opportunity up.

This was her shot to make a difference in the world. Her shot at making life bearable and safe for everyone. Nothing like placing the entire state or country upon her own shoulders; geez, who did she think she was, Superwoman? She took her time getting ready for work, choosing her clothing carefully, sipping her coffee slowly while Max weaved in and out of her legs. She attempted to compose her thoughts and the approach she intended to take when being interviewed. "Alright, Max, wish me luck!" With a pat on the head and a quick look around to make sure that Max had everything he needed for the day, she headed out the door.

The drive to work seemed to take forever and parking was ridiculous. What else is going to go wrong? she wondered. No, stop that train of thought right now. Everything will go smoothly. My coworkers will be thrilled. We'll get the job and make headlines.

Walking into the office, she saw that John was the only other person there. Breathing a sigh of relief, she made her way over to his office.

"Good morning, John. How are you today?"

"Well, hello Olivia, you sure are early today. What brings you to my door this fine morning?"

"John, they emailed me. The RED. They want to interview me and discuss my proposal."

"That's great, Olivia! I thought it sounded like a fine idea when you brought it to the table during our last meeting. So why the worried face?"

"This is huge, John. Am I ready for this? I've never headed up an operation before. That's what you do."

"I am sure that you will do a wonderful job. This was your brainchild. I just hope they allow you to keep it and see it through to the end if they decide to approve it."

"Approve what?" Dave asked, he and Sari making their way over to the office door, Claudia, another of Olivia's coworkers, not far behind.

"Great, all of you are here!" Olivia said. "I was hoping to catch everyone together. After I left the bar last night, I checked my emails, and both the RED and NED are interested in meeting to discuss my proposal." She meekly looked at her friends. "I didn't call anyone to tell them last night because I was still in shock, processing the possibilities that this could open for all of us. If they assign me to oversee the project, if they decide to back it, and if they let me choose my team. So many ifs, it's overwhelming really."

Wide-eyed looks, smiling faces, and words of encouragement all surrounded Olivia, her team obviously happy for her. She could now breathe a tiny sigh of relief.

Olivia felt Sari's dark almond-shaped eyes on her. "You should have called me immediately. Girl what is wrong with you?" Sari was always the one to pull her leg. "Haha. I'm playing with you. Why would you think that any of us would be upset that you didn't tell us sooner? You should know better than that kind of bullshit by now, especially with me, come on now."

Murmurs of agreement came from Claudia and Dave, both looking excited for her. "So, when is this fated meeting, Liv?" Dave asked curiously.

"It's at one o'clock this afternoon at the regional government building, so I will have to head over around noon. You know how parking can be over there. I might have to walk a mile."

Before a new round of conversation could begin John reminded them, "Off to work with all of you. We have a deadline for the last set of assessments coming up fast."

The next four hours dragged by so slowly for Olivia, time seeming to stand still, the pile of papers on her desk taking forever to whittle down. She felt like she was making no progress today, her mind full of concern thinking of the impending meeting. Looking at the clock yet again, she saw that it was almost time to head out. Finishing up one last detail on a recommendation, she packed up her belongings and headed toward the door, hearing words of encouragement as she left, wishing that Sari, or anyone really, were able to accompany her.

The twenty-minute drive to the state building ended up taking forty minutes. Thankfully, she found a parking spot on the same block as the entrance to the building.

Looking up at the immense building, butterflies began to fill her belly, and taking a shaky breath, she walked up the black marble stairs that led to a towering glass and iron doorway, the scrollwork of the iron curving beautifully, bringing out the beauty in the wavy colored glass. No expense had been spared when they built this mammoth building; it was exquisite. Walking into the arched entryway, Olivia looked up at the huge crystal chandelier hanging twenty feet above, shimmering, creating prisms all over the main hall. The beauty of this place was breathtaking and awe-inspiring, though also intimidating on a personal level.

These people that she'd been called to speak to were so high above her on the totem pole of life that she wasn't sure how she was going to keep the nervousness out of her voice. After checking in, she sat in an elegant armchair, looking at all of the wood scrollwork and plush mahogany fabric, realizing that they must be antiques because nothing was built like this anymore. She took in the art all around her, thinking that this place could double as a museum with all its beauty, antiques, and art. She was lost in thought, taking in the immensity of the room when her name was called, startling her slightly.

"Right this way, ma'am," said the plump office assistant, leading her down a long art-filled hallway. Anxiety spiking again, Olivia took a deep breath in hopes of calming her nerves and entered the modern-looking conference room. She took it all in. The décor was nothing like that of the main entrance and waiting areas. There was none of the antique or artsy feel in this room. It was all cold technology, things that served a purpose and nothing more.

Looking at all the faces before her, she felt as though she were on trial. Their eyes followed her as she made her way fully into the room, the weight of each of their stares a set of iron chains pulling at her, making her feel small and insignificant. She understood how Atlas must have felt carrying the world on his shoulders. There were seven people—four men and three women—all in a row, with one chair placed in front of them, meant for her. One of the women motioned to the chair in the center of the room. "Please have a seat."

"Thank you for viewing my proposal and inviting me here to speak with you in regard to it."

The woman in the center addressed her again, her nameplate reading Mrs. Hall. She seemed to be the spokesperson for the entire group. "It is an interesting, if not slightly controversial, idea that you have, Miss Titos. We would like to hear more about your vision and ask a few questions. If you don't mind of course."

"Please feel free to ask anything. I have very high hopes for this project if it is accepted."

"As I am sure you are now aware, this board is made up of both the RED and NED. This is not a project that can be put together by just the regional department. The sheer size and cost that it will incur is out of our reach. We have been concerned with which department will take the lead if it is indeed decided that a go-ahead will be given to your vision. The country has been looking for quite some time for a solution to the growing epidemic that is the drug scene, namely the drug Ink, which I am sure you are familiar with, and to the safety risks that are being posed to good citizens each and every day. Your idea may actually be able to make most people happy, or, at the very least, be tolerable to the general public. One of the only reasons that we are even considering this extremist proposal is that we have yet to make much headway with this dilemma, and the country wants results now. It may not be seen quite as controversial, though it is quite a radical idea, given the public is demanding that the government come up with a solution promptly."

"Yes ma'am, that is my hope, to enable the safety of our streets, but also allow for those caught up in drugs to live the life they choose, without posing harm to citizens who choose clean lives."

"So, you propose we send them to an island, one that has a temperate climate, to live out their days as they see fit, having access to the drug of their choice, food, shelter, and clothing, and having all their needs met. How do you propose the country pay for this?"

"If they choose to live on the island, the jail system will surely shrink. There will be less drug offenders on the streets, so you won't need as many officers on duty. Also, the health care system would ease due to lack of inmates. The reduction in the need for corrections officers will also save money. Some of those that qualify could be used as guards on the island to keep unauthorized visitors out. The main system used to keep people on and off the island would be security cameras and security systems. We employ those that are already adept at using these devices. Much like cameras used by hunters, the system would detect movement and alert those at the watchtower of a breach.

As a secondary measure we would have a security patrol to cover the island on regularly scheduled routes."

"Interesting. Please continue."

"Many people make poor choices while on drugs and commit crimes such as auto theft, burglary, and assault. If the drugs are taken out of the equation, I believe that we will see a dramatic decrease in these types of crimes as well, which again eases court costs, as well as policing and jailing. I realize that shifting these people to the island will not eradicate drugs from general society, but I can say with confidence that it will greatly diminish the amount that we see each day in our cities."

"Just to reiterate, not only will there be voluntary residents, but you are also proposing that instead of sending drug offenders to jail, we ship them off to this island where they'll serve out their sentences?"

"Yes, but not only that, we offer a contract to the people that have not been arrested or otherwise to go to the island voluntarily if they so choose, where they will be free to live their life as they see fit. The guards would only be on the island to make sure no one leaves or attempts to come ashore without permission." Olivia took a deep breath, continuing to try to make them see the value in her idea. "If they end up in prison they will eventually get out and return to the streets, but if they get the opportunity to choose life on an island the chances of them wanting to return to the mainland would be nearly nonexistent. Unlike a prison sentence where the addict would be unhappy and create more and more conflict, they would have a choice to live away from the scrutiny of society. In turn society gets to be rid of what they consider parasites to their way of life."

"Do you truly believe that people would voluntarily go to this island? How would we manage health care and the pregnancies that would come from so many poor choices being made, as I am sure that they would?"

"That will be one of the stipulations of the island: everyone that resides there must agree to voluntary birth control. Both men and women will be fitted with the birth-control implant, so there will be limited risk of unwanted pregnancies. Health care would be much the same as in our current jail system, though a bit more relaxed. If you look at the draft, it shows how many guards, nurses, and general workers would be needed to ensure a smooth-running system. The best way to envision the island would be to think of an assisted living community. There will be health care, living accommodations, simple forms of recreation, and food and nutrition all provided to the residents, as well as their daily portion of Ink. No one will be forced to stay on the island unless they have been sent over through the court system. However, once they leave, they will not be allowed back. I do not foresee that being an issue though. My belief is that once they get there they will stay."

"Yes, we did see that. Now, where are we going to get an island from? We do not have the financial backing to purchase an island."

"The government already owns several islands off the East Coast that would work quite well. There would be no need for purchasing, only for clearing and construction. I am sure that if the public were given the option of having safe, clean streets again, they would be more than willing to increase taxes a bit. Some organizations would likely be willing to donate time or money to this cause as well. It truly benefits everyone to implement this idea and move forward with this project. Imagine being able to walk safely to your car without the fear of being mugged or taking a chance on running into a drug deal gone wrong, or, as in the case of the last city assessment I was on, running into a naked woman standing on your front lawn and staring into your home on some unknown drug. To feel safe and live in a clean neighborhood would be amazing for those that don't get that luxury now. To be able to do so, while still addressing the needs and wants of those that choose to be consumed by drugs, would be just short of a miracle."

One of the men spoke, his voice deep and gruff. "Does this have anything to do with your own personal run-in with Ink, Miss Titos?"

Olivia's face paled considerably, reading the nameplate in front of the man that spoke and realizing that he was the head official for the NED. Swallowing her nerves, she responded, "What are you implying, Mr. Rhodes?"

"I do not imply anything. My statements are factually based. Did you think that we wouldn't do our research on you, given the enormity of this proposal, Miss Titos? Your previous fiancée, a Miss Aria Summers, award-winning journalist, became an addict of Ink when she went undercover to follow a story on said drug, correct?"

Taking a deep breath, Olivia replied, "I would be lying if I said that Ink hasn't affected my life in a negative way. It's also impacted me positively as well though. What happened two years ago has only fueled my passion to help make our streets safe and clean again, while not imposing an undesired life on another."

"And was that what you tried to do with Miss Summers? Impose a life on her that she did not want?"

"No Mr. Rhodes. I... let her go, so she could live the life that she chose."

"Understand this, Miss Titos: if you get the go-ahead for this project, and that is a big if," the man said, pausing to glare at her with hardened eyes, "I will personally be keeping a very close eye on your operation."

"I would welcome that, Mr. Rhodes," Olivia replied firmly, her shoulders relaxing just a bit. Relief swept through her at the cessation of the inquisition about Aria, the band across her chest that was squeezing the air out of her body released its death grip on her, and she was able to breathe deep again.

Mrs. Hall stepped in, saying, "Thank you for your time today, Miss Titos. We will let you know if we have any other questions or need of you."

Realizing that she was being dismissed, Olivia rose and said, "Thank you for your time," and walked out of the conference room.

She could feel a bead of sweat roll down the center of her back. Hoping that she had made a good impression, but feeling the nerves still making her stomach swim, she decided it was imperative to grab a quick bite to eat before heading back to the office. Her mind was still reeling from the line of questioning that she had received from Mr. Rhodes. Who would have thought that they would bring that up now?

6

⚛

She called John to let him know of her plan, but he told her to go ahead and take the rest of the day off since they were pretty much caught up at the office. She breathed a huge sigh of relief and turned her car toward home, wanting nothing but to take a relaxing bath and to wash this stress-induced sweat off her body.

Olivia went to her bedroom to gather her things to take a shower, knowing that if she were to take a bath, she would probably drown by falling asleep in the tub. After the quick shower, Olivia lay on her bed, wrapped in her towel, and began to go over the meeting and all the information the NED had relayed to her, but unintentionally drifted off to sleep, deeply exhausted...

Olivia found herself in the alley by the bar that she used to frequent soon after graduating from college, backed into a corner near a dumpster by a couple of guys, their intent blatantly showing in their body language. Mean laughter came from their mouths as they reached for her now, pulling at her clothes, grabbing her arms and legs. She tried to scream, but they shoved a dirty rag in her mouth, the smell of it making her gag, which they laughed about as they hiked her skirt high up over her thighs, exposing her panties. One man held her tight from behind while the other ripped her panties off brusquely. The first man moved to undo his zipper, his desire apparent by the bulge in the front of his pants. Olivia struggled as hard as she could but just couldn't seem to shake them off. Tears flowing freely down her face, she knew that they were going to have their way with her.

The man holding on to her loosened his grip briefly to rip open her button-down shirt, exposing her breasts before gripping her arms again even tighter than before. Leaning in, the first man whispered in her ear while pinching her nipple hard with one hand and forcefully shoving the fingers of his other hand deep between her legs. "Stop fighting, sweetheart, you're going to get the best fucking of your prissy little life tonight." He laughed and licked her face, leaving a trail of fetid-smelling saliva. Reaching down to grasp his erection, he positioned himself to forcefully enter Olivia's body. She continued to struggle and tried to scream, tears flowing down her face like rivers now.

Then a sudden loud crack echoed through the alley and the first man fell to his knees and then all the way to the ground. The second man, realizing that they were no longer alone, released her and took off running.

Falling to the ground, Olivia scrambled as far away from the unconscious man that lay on the ground as she could, whimpering and scared, clothing in tatters, trying to grip the pieces still left to cover her body. She looked up at her savior, looked deep into those dark brown almond eyes. "Oh my god, thank you, thank you for saving me," cried Olivia, breaking down into body-wracking sobs, unable to stop, but allowing Sari to come close and cover her with a jacket.

Olivia woke from the force of the sobs shaking her body, all the emotion coming to the surface, tears flowing down her face even in sleep. She had to take a few minutes to blink herself into full awareness, realizing that it was the middle of the night. She took in her surroundings: her king-size bed, the big bay window with floor-to-ceiling curtains, her mirrored closet doors. She was in her bedroom, not some dirty alleyway.

It was just a dream. Well, not just a dream. It was a memory, one that she tried not to think about now. She had gone to therapy and done her inner work. The memory had no power over her. All the stress that I've been under lately must have brought it to the surface. The feelings of helplessness and lack of control have been hovering recently.

It was a wonder that she was so comfortable being naked all the time after all that had happened to her, but other than making her more watchful, it hadn't changed much about her. Thankfully Sari had shown up to rescue her before that disgusting pile of garbage had been able to rape her. It had been close though. She had felt the tip of his erection against her body. Being here in her house naked didn't ever leave her feeling exposed, but that dream did, and she couldn't seem to shake it.

Knowing she needed to talk it out or at the very least share the burden, she did something she didn't necessarily want to do. She sent Sari a text that read, I had a nightmare. You know the one. If you aren't busy, could you come by? I don't want to talk about anything. I just need company. She waited for an answer for quite some time but received none.

It took a couple of shots of whisky before she decided that she was going to attempt to go to bed for the night, knowing she probably wouldn't sleep. She took one last drink and placed the glass in the dishwasher. She turned to walk down the hall to her room when a pounding on the front door made her jump a mile. Peeking out of the curtain, she could see Sari's Camaro in the driveway. With a sigh, she opened the door, a bathrobe wrapped tight around her body.

As soon as the door was closed and locked, Olivia found herself being carried to the bedroom in Sari's arms and placed gently on the bed. Sari began to get undressed, stripping down to just underwear and saying, "I know you're exhausted and won't be able to sleep alone, Liv. I'll stay with you tonight. I can even sleep under a different blanket if you want."

"No, I want to feel you. I don't want to be alone tonight, but I don't want..." Blushing deeply, Olivia looked at the ground.

"I know, babe. Come here and let me hold you." Sari slid into the middle of the bed under the sheets, arms extended toward Olivia.

They lay quietly for some time, Sari stroking Olivia's back and hair softly.

"I like the way that feels, your hands on me," Olivia said, "but why doesn't it make me want to have sex? What's wrong with me?"

"I thought you didn't want to talk tonight?"

Rolling over to face Sari, Olivia said, "But it makes you want sex; I can feel it in your body."

"You need to stop being so hard on yourself about this sex nonsense. You had some bad shit happen to you. I know that you will get over it someday."

"You know that it's not just that time in the alley when you saved me that's the problem, right?"

"Yes, I know where most of the problem is. It lies with Aria, and someday you will let it all go." Sari stroking Olivia's back slowly with her fingertips created cold chills that traveled through her body. Her nipples became erect, brushing against Sari's body.

"Last I heard she was out of the region working with drug runners."

"That really isn't surprising given how bad she was getting before you finally put her stuff to the curb," Sari said gently. "It might be time to talk about that night with Aria, if not to me, then to someone. It is possible that getting it out, saying the words, will release them from your body, so you can heal properly."

"You already know what happened, Sari. I don't want to relive it."

"But you are. Every time you try to feel anything sexual, you relive it and it creates a blockage in you. You are not broken, Liv. You are just blocked. It isn't a physical thing. Your body reacts to touch. It's a mental thing."

"I guess you might be right, but that means bringing everything back to the surface."

"Yes, it does, but then it might lose its hold on you. You told me the outline of what happened, but you never really shared the entire story with me."

"I've never shared the entire story with anyone, Sari."

"Which is why you need to get it out, so you can have your life back. Liv, it's been more than two years since it happened. It's time for a clean slate."

Yawning and feeling incredibly tired, Olivia rolled back over, pressing her body tight against Sari's body for comfort and heat. "You are probably right, but I'm too tired for that tonight."

Pulling Olivia even closer, Sari whispered, "I know, love," listening to her breathing deepening and slowing down as she drifted off to sleep. Sari continued to stroke Olivia's body, soft and slow across her abdomen, enjoying the feel of her so close... enjoying it a little too much honestly. Sari kissed the back of her neck gently, a soft moan coming out of Olivia's mouth as she whispered, "See, you still feel, we just have to get those subconscious thoughts out of the way." With her hands caressing and comforting Olivia's body soft and slow, Sari spoke softly, knowing that Olivia couldn't actually hear the words but needing to say them anyway. "I will do anything that I can to help you."

Sari held Olivia close and allowed sleep to come.

7

Late morning sunlight streamed through the window. Olivia mumbled a good morning as she rolled over, reaching for the arms that had held her all night and allowed her a blissful night of sleep. Realizing that she was alone left her feeling curiously bereft, though it was short-lived as her phone began to buzz incessantly until she picked it up.

"Hello Dave."

"Hey, I hope the meeting went well yesterday! I figured you could use a bite to eat. How about if I stop and grab Chinese for lunch and stop by your place?"

Stifling a sigh, Olivia shrugged to herself. Why not? "Sure, but give me an hour, okay? I need to get things cleaned up a bit."

"Yeah, no problem! See you in a while. You want General Tso's chicken with fried rice, right?"

"Oh my god yes, and add an egg roll please, I'm starving!"

The water felt amazing on her skin as it poured down over her head. She tried to let go of the worry about her proposal. What would be, would be. She had made her case, and she felt that she had done it well, so now it was in the director's hands. Getting out of the shower, she threw on a pair of shorts and a tank top, comfy but still appropriately dressed for company. Hearing Dave pull up out front, she pulled out some wine, glasses, ice, and brought them out to her enclosed back porch, calling out, "I'm around back on the porch."

"On my way. Do I get to meet Max now?"

Laughing, Olivia picked up the kitten as Dave stepped up onto the porch. "Meet my love, Max. He is already so much healthier than the night I saved him!"

"He is a cute one. How did the meeting go? Unless you don't want to talk about it."

"It's alright. It was intense, but I believe that I did my best to promote my idea and how it would benefit all the people of the country. I was surprised that the NED was there with the RED. Although, I guess it makes sense even though it doesn't happen often," she added hesitantly. "They asked about Aria."

"Wow! Are you okay? What did they say about her?"

Doing her best to avoid the topic of Aria, she replied, "It was quite intimidating. All of them stare at you, not saying a word except for the elected spokesperson, silently judging every word you are saying. I felt like I was on trial for a crime or something."

"I bet you did an amazing job, though. You never let on when something gets to you," he commented, letting the subject of Olivia's ex slip away.

"I try not to, anyway. What's been happening with you? It's been a while since we just hung out and talked."

"Not much. I did get that bartender's number like you suggested. Tammy is a bit of a handful. I'm not sure what to do about her. Besides, I still hold on to hope that you and I... well, you know."

"Dave, you have got to stop waiting for me. I don't want a relationship with anybody. I'm not in that place right now. I keep trying to tell you that we are and will always be friends."

"I know, it just feels like it could be more sometimes, Liv. I know you feel it too," Dave said as he placed his hand high on Olivia's thigh.

Removing his hand from her thigh, she spoke clearly. "I have no idea what you think I am feeling, Dave, but I am sure that you are misinterpreting it. I cannot be with anyone. I don't want to be with anyone."

"Fine. If you say so, Liv."

"So, about this bartender. What do you mean by she's 'a bit of a handful'? I said get her number. You know, talk, and get to know each other, not bring her home and play house."

"I know, and that's what I was trying to do."

"Then what's the issue?"

"It's kind of weird to discuss it with you, but you're pretty open-minded, so here goes. She sent me pictures of herself."

"Okay? What's weird about that? A lot of women like taking selfies."

"Here, I'll just show you."

Leaning over, Dave brought up the messages he'd exchanged with the bartender, Tammy. Somewhat surprised, Olivia saw a naked woman on the screen. "She sent you nudes? Let me see that." She took Dave's phone from his hand.

She took in the picture, a pretty brunette lying seductively on a bed, a bit overweight, long legs, heavy rose-tipped breasts, piercing blue eyes, with a sheet lightly draped over her hips, barely covering just her nether region. She swiped to the next picture, Tammy again, bottom lip caught between her teeth in a sexy way, now sitting on the edge of the bed and leaning toward the camera a bit, legs crossed, breasts falling forward, the rose-colored nipples standing out, beckoning, wanting to be touched.

Looking at Dave incredulously, she said, "If you don't know what to do with her, then I really don't know what to tell you."

"What if she sends that stuff to every guy who gets her number?"

"And? What if she were a model posing nude in a magazine? Would it be acceptable then?"

"Yeah, I guess I get what you are saying. It just caught me off guard, that's all."

"I get that, but that woman is so comfortable in her own skin it's sexy. She owns that shit. If you don't like her in that way, then fine, but don't criticize that kind of confidence by saying she is a handful. That woman is beautiful, and she knows it."

"It's just intimidating is all."

Laughing, Olivia asked, "Did you send her any pictures back? Haha."

Flushing and spluttering, he managed to get out, "No way! But are you sure there isn't any chance of us dating, Liv? I don't want to start something else if there is. I will wait for you if you just need time."

"Dave, I love you as a friend, but no, we are never going to date."

Olivia watched as Dave's face grew red and he looked away, swallowing loudly, his hands clenching slightly. She felt for him, but she was getting tired of having to constantly rebuke him. She gave him a moment to regain his composure before quietly saying, "I'm sorry. It's just how it is."

Clearing his throat to hide his emotion, Dave asked, "So, when are we going swimming at those underground caves that Sari mentioned last month? It's definitely warm enough now."

Knowing that he was not acknowledging her rejection, she replied anyway. "Not sure. You should find out when everyone is free so we can make the trip."

8

Weeks slipped by and time passed with no word on the proposal, creating a storm inside of Olivia. Maybe it's time to give up on it and just let go of the idea. Damn it, no! I know this is a good idea, no, a great idea. It can help so many people. Sure, there may be some resistance at first, but I am sure most people would eventually come around and see the merits. This way everyone would be able to live the life that they choose without having to harm anybody else. I know it can work and I could oversee the entire project, cost-cutting and saving where possible. If only they would give me a chance. But it's been three weeks and nothing, not even a tiny email saying that they are still going over schematics. Nothing. Not a word. All these thoughts drifted through Olivia's mind while sitting at the bar, staring off into space, her favorite chicken wings in front of her untouched.

She was brought back to reality by a hand waving in her face. "Hey, sugar! I asked if the wings were okay. You haven't touched them, and it's been a half hour," Tammy said with a concerned look on her face.

"Oh crap, I'm sorry, Tammy. I didn't mean to ignore you, just lost in thought. The wings are fine."

"They better be. Best damn wings in this city. But hey, since it isn't busy, do you mind if we chat for a bit?"

A surprised look crossed her face, but Olivia nodded, wondering what Tammy could possibly want to discuss with her. It wasn't like they were friends or anything. This was just the after-work spot that the group liked to come hang out at to grab something quick to eat and a drink or two.

"You work with Dave, right? At COST, the task-force place. He told me some stuff about it. It seems like a really important job."

"Yes. We work together."

"I feel kind of silly asking you this, but does Dave have a girlfriend or something?"

"Shouldn't you be asking him that, Tammy? It's not really my business or place to be answering questions like that."

"I mean it could be fun even if he did have one. Mhmm, yes it could." Catching the look on Olivia's face, Tammy said with a laugh, "My humor gets me in trouble sometimes. I've asked if he is seeing anybody and he says no, but then he does this back-and-forth thing. Like we are talking, and it seems to be going well, and then he backs off for a few days. It's just weird. I guess I'm wondering if I should just forget about it. He asked me out to dinner last week and then cancelled the day before. Something about getting caught up at work."

"I'm not making excuses for him, but last week was kind of crappy. We were all out in the field in a questionable area and some stuff went down. He may have needed time to come down from all of it. I'm sure he will tell you all about it when he gets a chance."

"Your work seems so exciting and fun. I wish I could do something like that, instead of tending bar, getting hit on constantly. It's like everyone, men and women, think that because I tend bar, I must be easy. They seem to think I go home with someone new every night I work."

Chuckling a bit, Olivia asked, "Well, are you? Not that it matters. Just curious. You can be easy or not and do whatever you want. It's your body and your life."

"No, I don't think I am at all. I really enjoy sex, but I've only given maybe three guys from here my number in the four years that I've worked here."

"Don't let anyone make you feel bad about liking sex or being comfortable with yourself and your personal choices."

"I actually dated one of those guys for about a year before he turned to drugs and I just couldn't live with him anymore."

Olivia drifted back into her own past. Picking Aria up off the floor, so high on drugs that she had no conscious idea of what she was doing. Olivia sitting there babysitting her to make sure that she didn't harm herself somehow or choke, watching and waiting.

"Hey Olivia, where did you go again? Are you alright? You really seem out of it lately."

"Oh Tammy, I'm sorry. I've had a lot on my mind. It's good that you managed to get out of that relationship. You don't want or need to live like that."

Shrugging, Tammy said, "It was rough for a while. He got into that drug Ink, and I tried to get him off it, but no matter how hard I tried, he kept going back to it. He said there was nothing in the world that made him feel so good. I just don't get it; how could he not see what he was doing to himself? I took a video of him one time and showed him. He got so mad and embarrassed that he slapped me across the face and said that I was a no-good whore who couldn't keep a real man if I tried. So, I kicked him out and never looked back. I really loved him though. That was one relationship that broke me down bad."

"Sounds like one hell of an awful ride, Tammy. I'm glad that you got out before he could do worse to you."

"Shit, listen, I don't know why I just unloaded all of that onto you. We barely even know each other. I'm sorry, it just came tumbling out," Tammy said, beginning to turn away, seeming ashamed of herself.

Olivia grabbed hold of her arm before she could get away and pulled her back to where she was standing on the other side of the bar. Half climbing on the bar, she pulled Tammy into an awkwardly positioned hug, squeezing tight. "Don't be sorry. You made it out of a horrible situation. I'm happy to listen and flattered that you chose to share your story with me. There is nothing at all to be ashamed of in your story or now." Taking her face by the chin, Olivia looked deep into Tammy's eyes, bright blue meeting bright blue. "Be proud of yourself, and know that I will always lend an ear and a shoulder if you need one."

"Alright, thanks for that," Tammy replied, a little breathless, blushing a slight rose color. "You have beautiful eyes, Olivia. Just saying."

"Thank you. They're a lot like yours," as Olivia said as she noticed the rose-colored blush, remembering the pictures that Dave showed her. She cocked her head a bit and thought that color of her flushed face likely matched her rose-tipped breasts.

"Silly question," Tammy said, "but when you were looking into my eyes, I sort of felt like you were going to kiss me. Did that thought cross your mind? I've never kissed a girl before, and I think my body may have reacted to it a little bit. God, that's so embarrassing. I don't even know why I just asked you that." Blushing even brighter now, Tammy looked down at the floor.

Chewing on her bottom lip, Olivia looked at Tammy's pouty lips for a moment, wondering what she would taste like. Would she be sweet like honey, or tangy like sour apple?

"Not that you aren't extremely attractive, but no, I wasn't going to kiss you, Tammy. You should really give kissing a woman a try though if your body reacted the way you say. You never know what you might enjoy if you don't put yourself out there."

Nodding at what Olivia had said, Tammy replied, "Maybe someday with the right person."

"Could you pack up my wings so I can take them home please? I need to head out to take care of my kitty. He is probably getting lonely. Sometimes I think I need to get him a friend."

"Sure thing, and thanks again for listening. Can we keep that kiss thing between us, though?"

"Absolutely. I would never betray someone's trust. As for Dave, I'm not sure what to tell you. Use your best judgement there."

As she walked out into the cool summer night, Olivia breathed a sigh of frustration. Between all this waiting to hear from the directors, the job itself, hearing Tammy's story which triggered memories of her past, and wondering what in the world Dave was up to, the weight on Olivia's shoulders was crushing her.

Well, I can do something about one part of this dilemma, anyway.

She pulled her phone out and sent a text to both Sari and Dave. Meet me at my house in thirty minutes. And a second quick text, No, this is not about the project.

During the short drive home, Olivia wondered why she felt compelled to dive into this area with her friends. Dave's relationship choices were not her business, and she had never really cared what he did. But she felt like there might be more going on with him, which was why she had also called Sari in. Besides, Tammy had pulled on heartstrings that Olivia had forgotten existed within her, so she kind of wanted to help her out too. The revelation that Tammy now had a curiosity about kissing a woman might throw Dave a bit off his game, but Olivia wasn't planning on telling him that anyway.

Pulling into her driveway, she saw that both of her friends were already there and probably out on her back porch. She went in the front door to deposit her wings in the refrigerator and feed Max. She was thrilled and amused by how quickly he was growing and the personality that he was developing. He had a vet appointment soon to finish up his shots and get neutered. She thought again about getting him a friend so he wasn't alone all day while she was at work. She made sure that Max was well cared for—after all, he was the love of her life—but he might like the companionship of another cat.

Grabbing glasses and a large bottle of wine, Olivia wandered out onto the back porch, hearing her two friends chat amicably, relaxed and at home sitting on the outdoor furniture. She set the glasses down and filled each halfway, lifting one. "Here's to friends, especially ones that drop everything and come over twenty minutes early." Laughter filled the air, stirring a deep happiness within Olivia.

"Cheers."

"Salud."

Drinking deeply and refilling her glass, both Dave and Sari looked at each other, surprised, and then back at Olivia. "Sweetheart, I know this waiting has been rough on you, but you may want to take it easy on the wine," suggested Sari, looking quietly concerned.

"Since when do you worry about stuff like that? I'm fine. I asked you guys to come over because I stopped at Jed's Bar and Grill to get wings and ran into Tammy. We chatted for a while."

Dave took a sip of his wine, looking at Olivia. "I know what you are going to say: I'm playing with the woman and that it's not right. It's just been a rough week, and well, those pictures. What if she wants me to start sending her some? I don't want to do that. I would feel like an idiot!"

"Pictures? What pictures?" Sari questioned curiously.

"Tammy sent him nudes like three weeks ago when he first got her phone number, and he didn't know what to do about it," Olivia said. "It sort of freaked him out."

"I still don't know what to do about it obviously!" Dave said.

"You still have them? I want to see what has you all twisted up in- side. They must be good!"

Olivia shook her head as Dave handed Sari his phone. "You didn't know what to do about them, but you kept them. Geez, Dave."

"Why in the world do these pictures freak you out, man?" Sari said. "They're as classy as nudes can get. I could have shown you some re- ally freaky stuff before my phone got stolen last month. Some girls get into some crazy shit when taking photos. It's like a release or an artis- tic form of expression for them or something, I don't know. I do very much appreciate art though." Chuckling, Sari said excitedly, "I wonder if they backed up onto my wireless hard drive. I never even thought of that until now."

"My biggest thing is what if she sends them to everyone?" Dave asked. "I don't know if I want to date a chick that everyone has seen naked in person."

"Dave, stop being such a judgmental douche bag. You sound like a prudish asshole right now."

"Exactly like an asshole. A hypocritical one as well," Sari said. "I've seen Olivia mostly naked and yet you still want to crawl up in all of that."

Olivia swatted at Sari. "What the fuck, you're an asshole too! You may have seen me basically naked, but we never did anything; besides, there were extenuating circumstances that day. It's not like I intentionally got naked in front of you. I was covered in someone else's body fluids and needed to get clean. God!"

It was when she had first started working for COST; they had been placed together. They were always a good team. Their boss at the time had sent them out to test them in a particularly bad area a couple of hours away. He was such a power-hungry jerk. Both of them were happy the day he got fired and John replaced him. Here they were, just the two of them, one brand new to the job, walking the streets in a dangerous, drug-filled area, trying to remain professional and go unnoticed. Yeah, right.

Even dressing down, they stood out like a sore thumb in that neighborhood. Some junkie came up and started harassing them for money, willing to do anything for just a twenty-dollar bill. They tried to get him to move along and leave them alone but to no avail. When they had just about reached their rental car, the guy threw himself at Olivia, grabbing hold of her, trying to get into her pockets to steal whatever he could find. Before Sari could get to the man, he had started retching all over Olivia, still grabbing at her the entire time he was spewing his insides all over her.

Finally, Sari managed to toss the man away from Olivia, who was now covered in vomit, and who knew what else, standing there in anger and shock. They made it back to the hotel, trying to keep the rental as clean as possible, rushing into their shared room. Olivia had begun ripping the clothes from her body, throwing them in the garbage, and immediately took a scorching hot shower in an attempt to wash away the putrid smell of that man and the disgust that she felt at his vomit on her body, the scent dragging her back to the days of caring for Aria and always cleaning up after her. After showering, Olivia had to walk back into the bedroom almost naked, not realizing in her rush that the towels were only a bit larger than hand towels. Plus, she had never taken clean clothes into the bathroom to use to get dressed.

Sari had watched her get dressed quietly, though appreciatively, taking in Olivia's honey-colored skin, smooth curves, and perky yet full breasts, feeling her desire growing, but saying only, "I don't know how someone hasn't snatched you up and made you theirs."

Olivia's response had been simple and direct. "That's because I'm not a possession to be had, Sari. You know that."

As Olivia's mind drifted back to the present, she heard Dave say, "I would be lying if I said I wasn't jealous of you for that, Sari."

Eyes rolling hard, Olivia was slightly irritated and spoke firmly. "Goddamnit, let's focus here. Is everything okay with you, Dave? It's not like you to be so wishy-washy about a good-looking woman that is so obviously into you."

"I'm all good, guys, really. I just want to make sure she is into just me and not a bunch of other people too, I guess."

Laughing and slapping Dave on the back, Sari said, "How the hell are you going to find out any of that if you keep avoiding her, man? She is a sweet little number, all baby blues and brown hair, and she mixes up a killer mojito! If it's not just about looks for you, she is also super sweet and a good conversationalist. I've sat and talked with her a few times over the past couple of years."

Olivia smiled to herself as the conversation flowed on. There was nothing like having good friends that could razz you or put you in your place. Thankful for her friends, she raised her glass again. "Here's to great friends and great times!" They raised their glasses together, drinking deeply and smiling at each other like idiots. Refilling everyone's glasses, Olivia thought to herself, *Thank goodness it's a Friday, because the way we are going, everyone is crashing here.*

"You guys are right," Dave said. "I am going to give it a go with Tammy."

"Hell yes, I will drink to that!" Sari exclaimed, raising her glass. "Time to break out another bottle, babe!"

9

The scent of coffee and bacon drifted through the house, rousing its guests from their slumber. As if that were not enough to wake Sari and Dave, Max was tearing through the hallway, sounding like a herd of elephants, zooming this way and that. He fled back down the hall and into the kitchen, where Olivia smiled softly, cooking breakfast for everyone, happy to take on a nurturing role. She loved to cook and had missed making meals for other people. The breakfast spread was almost ready when Dave made his way to the kitchen table, finding a mug of coffee waiting for him, and a second mug for Sari next to it.

"You are heaven sent, Liv," mumbled Dave, taking a huge gulp of coffee.

"What is this delish smell tantalizing my senses, Liv?" Sari asked, grabbing the mug of black coffee.

"I figured that I would make breakfast for all of us since I gave you far too much wine and you both got stuck staying the night."

"I wouldn't call it an inconvenience, babe; your guest rooms are to die for. Those beds just swallow you up and the pillows suck you right in, not to mention how soft your sheets are. Maybe you should run a bed-and-breakfast in a cute little tourist town once we get the state cleaned up!"

"That is a great idea, Sari, if I wanted to bust ass for the rest of my life. Those inn owners work so hard, and I like what I do now most of the time. I shouldn't even be saying this out loud, but with any luck and a bit of patience maybe they will approve my proposal and then I can oversee the entire project."

"So, are we in on this project if you get to choose your team?" Dave asked meekly.

"What!? Are you crazy? Of course, you guys are! We have been a team for the last year. Nothing is going to change that. Except that I will be the boss. Boy will that be different."

"It's a good thing she isn't power-hungry, Dave, or we would all be in trouble, man!"

Suddenly a pop song began playing, followed by loud buzzing.

"Who would be trying to get a hold of me so early on a Saturday since both of you are right here?" wondered Dave.

Olivia started to bring food over to the table. "Well go get it and check," she said, setting down a heaping pile of bacon, a huge plate of scrambled eggs, stacks of pancakes, a dish of breakfast sausage, maple syrup, butter, and a carafe of fresh coffee.

"You outdid yourself, Liv. I think you should marry me and cook for me every day," Sari said.

"Give me a break, Sari; you won't ever get married, and I know you too well to marry you anyway. Dig in before it gets cold!" Olivia shouted down the hall. "You too, Dave."

Walking into the room slowly, looking at his phone, Dave said, "How can she work so late at night and be up so early?"

"I assume that you are talking about Tammy, and it's really not that early Dave, it's already ten o'clock in the morning. Now eat. I didn't make all of this food for it to go to waste."

"She wants to hang out today if I'm free."

"Well, you are free today," Sari said. "Or are you planning on using Liv and I for an excuse, Dave?"

"I have a better idea!" Olivia said. "Why don't we all hang out today? None of us has anything pressing to do. We discussed that last night. We should go check out those caves that we have been talking about for months now. We can explore and swim. It will be a great time, and then you won't be so self-conscious being alone by yourself on an actual date with Tammy," Olivia suggested excitedly.

"Are we all riding together or meeting there?" Dave wondered out loud.

"I haven't even agreed to go, guys," Sari said abruptly.

Batting her long thick eyelashes and gazing at Sari with her bright blue eyes, Liv pouted. "Pretty please? We all need a day of fun. We haven't done anything like this since we drove to the beach like a month ago and we said we would do it at least every other week."

"Yeah, but this will feel like babysitting, Liv. I don't want to babysit Dave on a date."

Glaring at Sari and Liv, he said, "I don't need a babysitter. I only agreed because it would be cool for all of us to hang out and I've been wanting to go swim at the caves for quite a while now."

"Fine, but Dave takes his own car with Tammy or has her meet us there, and Liv and I will ride together," Sari said. "You never know what will happen, Dave, you might end up back at her place or vice versa. I'm driving my car. Liv those are my terms, take them or leave them."

Squealing with delight, Olivia hugged both of her friends. "I can be ready in about an hour. Does that work for you guys?"

"Better make it two hours," Dave said. "I need to go shower and shave before we go. I want to make a good first impression, right?"

"It's going to take you that long to get showered and shave, seriously? Whatever, Dave, go do your thing. So, we will meet at the caves' parking area at three o'clock, okay?" Olivia confirmed.

"That works for me. See you guys there. I will pick Tammy up so she doesn't have to drive all the way there. It's weird that she has a Saturday off." Grabbing another piece of bacon, he shoves it in his mouth before waving and walking out the door.

"Alright sweet thing, I am going to go home and get cleaned up. I will be back in a while. Maybe we could chill out here for a little while before we leave for the caves. Some of your homemade lemonade would be killer in this heat."

"I can do that. I just bought lemons a couple days ago. I must have known you were going to want some soon."

Sari grabbed Olivia by the waist and pulled her in for a tight hug and a kiss on the cheek, holding her close for a moment longer than necessary, heads resting together, dark hair mixing with dark hair. "Mmm, I got to go before I start wanting more than I should with you and your hot self, Liv. See you soon, babe."

Olivia waved and watched Sari walk to that sweet, sexy Camaro, get in, and drive away. She wondered to herself, Why don't I feel sexual attraction to anyone at all? I am constantly surrounded by good-looking people and yet, I feel no desire for any of them. Is there something wrong with me?

10

The drive down to the caves was comfortable and uneventful; they saw Dave's car already there when they pulled in. Tammy was leaning against the hood of Dave's car, laughing at something he was saying. Olivia smiled to herself. *Looks like they are hitting it off after all.*

"I see that smile, Liv; don't get your hopes up too soon for the happy couple. Don't go playing matchmaker either. Let it flow between them. It will be interesting to see how well she fits with him," Sari chuckled, eyeing Olivia knowingly.

Waving to them as she got out of the car, Olivia pulled her wrap closer around her body, not liking to be stared at by a bunch of people. They all met up by the entrance, purchased tickets, and began the descent into the caves. There was a dimly lit stairwell down which they had to make their way carefully, the rock walls damp and cool, the air surprisingly clean and fresh blowing up from the caverns below. "It doesn't seem like there are many people here today," Olivia pointed out.

"The better for us!" Dave stated, winking at Tammy.

Olivia raised her eyebrows, surprised at the familiarity that came so quickly between Dave and Tammy, thinking it was funny that just last night, he had been so worried about making a connection with this woman. Chuckling to herself, Olivia looked over her shoulder and caught Sari watching with interest as she walked down the stairs.

Olivia swatted at Sari, shaking her head, and turned around and saw the most amazing sight. They had stepped out onto a platform that led to the clearest, most beautiful blue-green water she had ever seen. The entire group just stared, taking it all in, the over fifty-foot-high ceilings of the cavern, the walls so colorful with all the different minerals running through them, everything shining and damp, beauty everywhere the eyes could see. Olivia exclaimed, "I want to stay here forever!" Everyone nodded in agreement.

As always, Sari broke the spell, saying, "I bet it looks even better from the water. Let's jump in!"

The group set their belongings down on a bench near the platform, stripping down to their swimsuits. Olivia checked Tammy out in her bright pink bikini, giving her silent props for being brave enough to wear one, even though she was a little on the chubby side. Olivia wondered to herself, If I weren't broken, would I be attracted to her? Would I want to touch her the way that Dave is, hand resting on the small of her back, slowly sliding lower, bodies touching, the attraction between the two obvious to everyone around them? A scream broke her out of her thoughts as she watched Tammy fly into the water, pushed by Dave, who jumped in almost on top of her. Playful squeals and laughter erupted from the water's edge.

"Let's go, Liv. If you're scared I'll let you hold my hand to jump in," Sari said.

"Stop it, you jerk. I can get in all on my own. Go ahead, jump in, you first!"

Sari laughed and did a perfect dive, forever the show-off. Olivia laughed, seeing Tammy looking on while quite impressed and Dave glowering. She moved to the edge, looking down into the beautiful water and the bottom covered in sand and stone twenty feet down. She dove down deep, swimming hard for the bottom. Once she reached it, she grabbed a handful of sand and kicked hard towards the surface. Her lungs were about to burst, gasping for air as she emerged from the depths, sand still in her hand. "I did it," she said with a smile, and showed them all. They all cheered for her and watched the sand slowly drift back to the bottom, swirling as it traveled downward, the hypnotic motion of the sand pulling them all in until it reached the depths. Swimming through the cavern, they were all in awe. It was so massive, so beautiful, so ancient.

Tammy swam up to Olivia and whispered, "I don't know if you said anything to Dave or not, but if that's why he finally decided to hang out with me, I wanted to say thanks."

"I really didn't say much. He is really into you. Anyone can see it."

They made their way to the shallower water where they could touch the bottom and relax while watching Dave and Sari see who could dive down the deepest and stay under the longest.

"So, are you and Sari a thing?" Tammy asked.

"No, we are not. We are good friends, like Dave and I, but that's all. Nothing romantic."

"Oh okay. Cool. About what we discussed the other day, if I wanted to try it out, would you maybe, umm do you think it would be possible, ah..."

"What are you trying to ask me, Tammy? It can't be that big of a deal."

"Shit, alright. Olivia, I'm only asking because I feel like we have some sort of connection and I trust you. You were so nice about my past and offered to talk or whatever if I needed... I don't want to ask some random person... Would you kiss me, like really kiss me, so I can experience it and maybe figure out if I am into women? I don't even know if you are, but it's just a kiss, and I think I can trust you. It would just be nice to know, ya know? Like not right now obviously, I wouldn't want to do that in front of people, especially Dave, but sometime. Would you, please?"

"Are you being serious right now? Oh my goodness, you are. Umm. Let me think about it, okay? I don't feel comfortable rushing into an answer right now," Olivia said, her thoughts drifting to green eyes and honey hair, full lips hot on her own, Aria ever pliant under her capable mouth.

"Okay, I totally respect that! Thank you for even considering it," Tammy gushed before turning to swim back to Dave. Once she reached him she began winding herself seductively around his body. Olivia and Sari watched as she wrapped her legs around his waist while he cupped her behind, pulling her body tight to his.

"What was that all about, Liv?"

"Jesus, Sari, did you hear any of that conversation? Good god, she wants me to kiss her so she can figure out if she likes women as well as men."

Laughing deeply, Sari pulled Olivia close. "You always manage to get yourself into these predicaments, but somehow you always manage to get out of them too. Maybe it can work in your favor somehow."

"I fail to see how that could possibly work in my favor."

"I'm not sure either, but that's just how it always seems to happen, babe. So, are you going to lock lips with her?"

"I don't know if I should. I understand her wanting to know and all, but Dave is my friend, so kissing her just seems kind of wrong."

"If you wait until they are officially dating, then it would be wrong, but they aren't, and I'm thinking she wants to find out before that happens."

"I'm not a guinea pig, and I have no desire to kiss anybody, male, female, or otherwise. I don't think there is anything sexual in me anymore."

"I think you are wrong about your sexuality; you are still healing, Liv. Hey, you never know, maybe being her guinea pig will wake something up inside you. If it doesn't, that's okay too. I just want to see you happy, babe, one way or another."

"Thanks Sari. I'm incredibly lucky to have you as a friend, my best friend really. Just don't tell Max. He would get upset, haha. Let's go dig into those sandwiches and spy on Dave," Olivia said, giggling and swimming toward the platform. "Come on," she said, beckoning Sari to follow.

"I will always follow you, Liv," Sari said quietly, so that the words couldn't be heard by anyone. "Always."

11

Walking into the office that Friday just felt too difficult for Olivia as she felt the warmth of the sun on her face. The birds sang their songs, so lovely to hear, and the breeze was warm but cooled the heat of the sun on her skin. The scent in the air spoke of beaches, relaxation, fun, and freedom. Working on days like today should be illegal, especially working inside an office with not enough windows to see the beauty of the day going by. Shrugging her shoulders, she sighed, taking one last longing look at the perfect day, and entered the COST office building, wondering if anything exciting would happen today. She doubted it. She still had not heard from anyone on her proposal and subsequent meeting, so that was most likely dead in the water. Even though she was feeling sullen about the entire situation, she called out, "Good morning," to the staff that was already gathered near John's office, complaining about having to work on such a beautiful day.

"Don't we have any field assignments for today, John?" Claudia asks.

"Not for a couple of weeks, sorry. On that Monday, our team will be headed to the southern part of the region for four days. We already have hotel accommodations taken care of. Claudia, you and Olivia will share a suite, and Dave and I will share a room. I figure we only need one suite since we can meet there for coffee in the mornings to discuss the plan each day. Sari will be staying back this time to hold the fort down."

"That's a long trip, John. I can see why you are trying to cut costs on the rooms. How many cities are you canvassing?" asked Sari.

"Why do you get to stay back?" griped Dave, only partially playful.

"We will be covering one city and three suburbs of said city," John said. "Dave, stop whining. At least I made sure we'll have double beds to sleep in instead of singles."

Claudia smiled. "I am actually kind of excited for this trip. I've never bunked with anyone on our trips before."

"Olivia and I usually bunk together since we have been friends forever and used to be roommates," Sari explained. "Bring earplugs, because she snores."

"I do not!" Olivia cried out indignantly.

"Oh, I never knew that you had been roommates!" Claudia said. "How cool. It's totally cool if you snore, I don't mind. I am simply happy to be bunking with someone, instead of being alone. I always get sort of creeped out in hotels by myself. It's stupid, I know, but I can't seem to help it."

"Apologies for that, Claudia. I wasn't aware of how you felt. I will make sure you always bunk with someone from now on," John stated, murmurs of agreement coming from the group.

Dave put his arm around Claudia's shoulder. "I can chase your monsters away if you want," he said, squeezing lightly and winking before walking to his desk. The action caused Claudia to blush, not sure how to respond.

It was at that moment that Olivia's phone chimed, alerting her to a new incoming email. The tone was one set for urgent messages only, so she opened it immediately, a feeling of hope and fear at war within her. She walked away from the group as she read the email twice to be sure of what it was saying.

Good morning Miss Titos,

We are pleased to inform you that both the RED and the NED have decided to accept your proposal on a conditional basis. We would like to schedule a meeting to further discuss the trajectory of this project...

She gripped the wall for support as John looked over, concerned.

"Are you okay, Olivia?" he asked.

A little breathless, she responded, "Yes. I am more than okay. RED and NED want to accept my proposal and discuss the next steps with the project. They want to schedule another meeting."

Whoops and hollers filled the office space as everyone cheered at the news. "This is something worth celebrating for sure," Sari said with an infectious exuberance.

The joy of the moment went quiet within Olivia as her intrusive thoughts moved to the forefront of her mind. Nothing good has ever worked out for me. Even now Aria haunts my every step, forever intertwined with my life.

A tear rolled slowly down Olivia's face, unnoticed by all those around her.

<h1 style="text-align:center">12</h1>

Olivia stirred in her bed, the sheets tangled all around her body. Rolling over to look at the clock, she saw that it was only eight o'clock in the morning, and on a Saturday, when she didn't even need to be up early. She was going to the shelter later to possibly find a friend for Max, but that wasn't until late morning.

Letting her mind drift backward in time, to another morning like this one, all the light coming in the windows, the sun soaking into her skin, warming and relaxing, another set of hands roaming her body, trying to memorize every detail, every curve and crevice... Honey-colored hair tickled her body as lips trailed down her neck, over her chest, drawing slow tongue circles, in no rush to go anywhere. They had spent hours in bed that morning. The only thing that mattered was a slow, soft pleasure. *Oh Aria, we had something so amazing. Why did you have to get caught up in that mess, just for the possibility of a huge headline?*

The sun warming her body while she lay alone in bed with the memory of Aria humming in the air, feeling only a slight tingle of what could possibly be her libido kicking in, Olivia dragged herself back to reality. She thought about how she used to have such a high sex drive, until the day that she broke. She wondered if she would ever heal and feel desire surging through her body again.

Rousing herself from the bed and her disappointing thoughts, Olivia wandered to the kitchen and looked out over her kingdom. She pondered taking a swim before jumping in the shower, looking at the glistening water, so beautiful and relaxing. She had worked so hard to make this place her home, her sanctuary. No, not just hers but Aria's as well.

Until that fateful night when her entire world had shattered into a million pieces. No point in thinking about it; it wouldn't change what happened.

Her phone rang from the kitchen counter, her favorite song bumping along, beckoning her to answer. She slowly got to her feet, walking back in the house to see who was calling so early. Surprised to see that it was Dave, she answered with a cheerful hello.

"Hey Liv, I'm glad that I didn't wake you. I had a question for you. I know that we are all supposed to come over to your place tonight, but I wanted to let you know that Tammy had to pick up the late shift because someone called out or something."

"Okay, that's not a big deal. Is that the only reason you called?"

"No, not really. I was wondering if I could come over early, so we could talk. I need your opinion on some stuff, but I don't want to discuss it in front of everyone."

"By 'everyone' you mean Sari?"

"No, well I mean yes, but Claudia too."

"Right, I forget that she seems to be part of the crew now. Yeah, that's fine. Come over around four o'clock. That will give us about an hour before the others arrive."

"You are the best, Liv! Thanks so much. See you tonight."

"Later, Dave." Olivia hung up the phone, wondering what in the world he could possibly want to talk to her about, especially alone.

Looking at the time, wondering how she'd lost an hour, she realized that she didn't have time for a swim before heading to the shelter. Deciding to shower later, before everyone came over, she grabbed jean shorts and a tank top to throw on before heading out. She grabbed the kitty carrier and blew Max a kiss as she walked out the door, promising to bring back the best friend he could ever want.

Walking into the shelter, Olivia greeted the attractive young man behind the counter warmly, stating her appointment time and what she was hoping to find.

"Hello Olivia, I'm Joe. Thank you for considering opening your home up to one of our rescues. We have a wide variety of animals for you to choose from, myself included if you are interested," he said with a laugh and wink.

Olivia found herself grinning at the comment, her interest slightly piqued. "I do have a fairly large home, more than enough room for a couple of pretty creatures."

He smiled broadly, coming around to open the door for her. "I'm not sure that I've ever found being called pretty as invigorating before now. I think I like it." He smiled broadly as he held the door, bringing her to the back area where they kept the cats and kittens.

"I do like pretty things," she commented, surprising herself with her boldness. As she walked around the corner she became overwhelmed with emotion when she saw how many cats there were in cages, all different colors and sizes, staring out at her, pleading to be petted or given attention.

"Do you see any that stand out?"

"I just don't know. This is so overwhelming. I wasn't expecting so many cats to be here to choose from. I just want to take them all home."

"I hear that often. Someday someone will take me home too."

"They will be lucky to do so, I'm sure," Olivia giggled, feeling a slight spark of intrigue light up inside her.

"Once we get you set up with a kitty, maybe we can discuss other possibilities," Joe said suggestively. "Until then, do you have any age or color preference?"

"I have a kitty at home that is between eight months and one year old right now, so it would need to keep up with him. As much as I would love to save a senior, I think Max would be too much for one.

He is highly active. Are there certain colors of cats that get adopted less than others?"

"Black cats get adopted much less than other colors. People seem to adopt both orange and white cats the most."

"Then I would like to see all of the black cats that would get along with my Max, please."

"Sure thing. It would be my pleasure." He led her to a room with a chair and many cat toys to choose from. He motioned for her to go in and have a seat.

Olivia made herself comfortable as Joe began bringing in all the black cats that seemed to be around Max's age. After he set the fifth one down, he said, "That's all that fit your request. Would you like me to stay with you while you play with them and decide? I know their histories if you are curious about them."

Smiling up at him, Olivia responded, "Yes, that would be lovely. I appreciate that. I don't want to interfere with your job at the front desk, though."

Winking, Joe said, "No worries, there is a buzzer at the front for people if someone isn't at the desk. It will sound through the whole building, so I will hear it no matter where I am, and right now I am happy to be here helping you."

"Wonderful! Can you tell me the story about the one with the crooked ear, please?" Time flew by as Olivia listened to each cat's story, Joe's voice a balm to her chaotic mind. He was a handsome man, athletic in build with beautiful eyes and warm smile. At first Olivia found herself wondering what it would be like to feel his full lips on hers. She wrinkled her nose like she smelled something gross and chided herself for such a ridiculous thought. Like he would even want to kiss her anyway.

Blushing at her thoughts, she looked down at her watch and gasped, realizing that she had been there for two hours already, just chatting and playing with the cats. "I am so sorry that I took up so much of your time! You must be so far behind on your work now!"

Standing up quickly, scanning the cats, trying to decide which one to choose in a hurry.

"Hey now, slow down. I really enjoyed spending time with you and playing with the cats. Plus, I don't want you making a rushed decision."

"Thank you, but I am fairly sure that I have made my choice, I will take that little girl over there, the one that stays to herself. I can just tell that Max and I will love her."

"Alright, that sounds like a good choice; just remember that she may be pregnant. We haven't gotten her checked for that yet, but she has already had all her shots."

"I know, and if she is, I guess we'll cross that bridge when we get there. Thank you so much for all your time; it was nice chatting with you."

"How about getting dinner together sometime?"

Eyes widening at the suggestion, Olivia took a step back.

"Maybe. Or possibly lunch. I'm not sure. My schedule is a little crazy right now."

"Oh, of course! Here's my number if you ever want to go out or even just chat about the cats."

Smiling gently at Joe, she picked Molly up. She had named her already and was placing her in the kitty carrier. "Thank you again." Olivia walked out of the shelter smiling to herself and thinking it was already a wonderful day!

When she walked back into her house, she was a little nervous that Max and Molly wouldn't hit it off. Olivia called him and heard him tear down the hall from one of the guest rooms. He zoomed around the corner and up onto the back of the couch, clearly excited that his mom was home. He stopped and stared at the cat carrier, curiously sniffing, nose to nose with Molly. He began to purr, noticing that the other cat was afraid. Breathing a huge sigh of relief, Olivia opened the carrier and Molly slowly emerged, looking back and forth, taking in her new surroundings. Max gave her space, sticking close, but not rushing or crowding her. He seemed to be okay with watching her explore. Olivia let Max handle giving Molly the tour of the house, needing to shower and get ready for everyone coming over in a few hours. Then she remembered that Dave had wanted to stop by early to talk, so she needed to get moving.

She chose a new sundress that flowed freely around her body, the fabric soft on her freshly showered skin, the colors making her tanned skin seem to glow. The style of the dress hugged her body in all of the right places, accentuating her breasts and behind enticingly. As she spun around in front of the mirror, she decided that she looked sexy and wondered what Joe would think of her in this dress. Surprised by her train of thought yet again, she rolled it around in her mind for a bit before going and putting the finishing touches on everything.

Olivia made sure that everything was ready to go before four o'clock so she could give Dave her undivided attention. Checking her reflection in the full-length mirrors on her closet doors one last time, she noticed Max and Molly curled up together on her bed, tails wrapped around each other, knowing that she had made the right choice in getting another cat warmed her heart.

A knock on the front door had her wistfully looking at her kitties before leaving the room to answer. She saw Dave with a couple of bags in his hands and a worried look on his face. Swinging the door open wide, Olivia motioned for him to come in, Dave's eyes going wide at the sight of her in the dress.

"My god, you are stunning, Olivia. My mind went completely blank when I saw you."

"I'm just a woman in a pretty dress, Dave, that's all. Thank you, though. What do you have here?"

"I brought chicken wing dip and tortilla chips for us to snack on later when everyone gets here. Listen, I really appreciate you letting me come over to talk."

"No problem at all. What's going on?"

"It's Tammy. I just don't know what to do or what to think about her. She is so free-spirited or something. I just don't get why she doesn't want to commit to a relationship, especially when we spend almost every day together now."

"Come on, let's go sit outside, this is too perfect of an evening to be wasting. Grab us each a beer from the fridge and you can tell me the whole story," Olivia suggested as she walked out to the back porch and sat in her favorite comfy chair, feeling the velvety fabric on her legs and bottom as she sat down, curling her legs underneath her.

Handing Olivia her drink, Dave sat next to her, popped the top, and took a long swig before returning to his story. "Whenever I ask her if she wants to make our relationship official, she says that she is finding herself right now and that she doesn't want to be unfair to me while she does that, so it's best if we just see each other for now. She actually told me that she was cool with it if I saw other women right now. I don't know what to do with that. I mean, if I'm being honest with myself, that is sort of cool to be able to see multiple women, but I doubt any other woman would be cool with that."

"You would probably be surprised at how many would be understanding about that, Dave, as long as you are honest about it, and it gives you a chance to figure out if you really care about her, instead of just jumping in headfirst because that's what society says you are supposed to do. It's better to take things slow for now. Tammy must have stuff going on that she needs to figure out, so be the decent guy and let her. Besides, if she decides that she doesn't want a relationship at this point in her life, it's better that you don't expect one with her."

"Yeah, but what if I start seeing another woman, I fall for her instead, and then Tammy decides she wants to be with me? Then I end up being the bad guy because I fell in love with someone else."

"That is not at all true. You need to decide what you want in life, Dave, not what you think life should look like. Have fun and enjoy the ride; this is the only one we get. Maybe seeing you go on a date with someone else will make Tammy realize that she wants to commit to you, or maybe she will be cool with it. You could also just stop seeing her all together, since it seems to be stressing you out just as much as you are enjoying it."

"I think I'll just stick it out and see what happens." Dave looked at the ground and quickly asked, "Liv, do you want to go out on a date with me?"

"Don't go there again, Dave. Please," Olivia emphasized. Hearing her phone go off, she picked it up from the table next to her, looked at the screen, and went pale.

"Liv, hey Liv, are you alright? What's wrong? Who is the message from?"

Barely able to croak out the words, Olivia replied, "It's an email. From the directors of NED. They want me to submit my portfolio. They are going to be conducting interviews for the director's position of the project. They are considering me as an applicant for the position since it was my idea!"

Olivia squealed happily as Dave picked her up joyously and twirled her around and around in the air.

13

Olivia began thinking about the week to come, the one she had to get through before her fated meeting with the agencies. She was just about packed for the week, four long days of fieldwork, only needing to gather some last-minute items like her toothbrush and other toiletries.

Walking into the bedroom, she saw her beloved Max cleaning Molly, licking her face and ears, so much in love with her, and Molly loving him right back. This was something that she had definitely gotten right. She was much happier leaving knowing that they would have each other to love on while she was gone. Laughing to herself, she wondered how they were going to feel about sharing the bed with her again when she got back from her trip since they all shared the bed at night now, even though each cat had their own fancy kitty bed on the floor near the big bay window.

Checking the time, she finished packing her items, double-checking that she had everything that she needed, and brought her suitcase to the front door. John would be picking everyone up with the work van this morning to make things more efficient. She went over the list that she had left on the kitchen counter for her house sitter, who was sleeping soundly in one of the guest bedrooms, to make sure everything was in order. She checked to see if the cats had enough food and water and finally sat back content that everything was situated and under control. She may be a bit of a control freak, but at least things got done and done the correct way. She knew that Hannah would call her once a day to provide her with an update on how things were going at the house.

Hannah had a regular job as well, but she enjoyed house sitting for Olivia because she had the place to herself, instead of sharing an apartment with her two friends, so it was a nice break and Olivia paid her well. Not once had Hannah given Olivia a reason to question her honesty or reliability, so she knew the house and cats were in trustworthy hands. Hearing the big gray van pull up out front, she grabbed her bags with one final look around and headed out the door, locking it on the way out for safety. Her motto was, "Always better safe than sorry."

John rolled down the passenger side window and called out, "Hop in the front, you're my first stop this morning."

Climbing into the passenger seat after stowing her bags in the back of the van, Olivia looked questioningly at John. "Why am I first today? You always get Dave before me."

"I wanted to have a minute to talk with you alone. We never get the chance, and I feel that it's important, especially now. The directors contacted me regarding you and your proposal, asking a lot of questions."

"Well damn. Alright, what did they say?"

"They wanted to know how competent you were in the field and as a team leader. Olivia, I really think that they are going to give the go-ahead for this project to start soon. They asked me what I thought of it and if I would be interested in having a hand running the project, like a partner. I told them that it was not my idea or proposal, so no, I would not want that opportunity."

"John! You would be great for it, and I could learn so much more from you."

"I understand that, but it was your proposal. You should be running the team and facilities on your own."

"What if they don't let me do it on my own?"

"What if they do? You have another opportunity to meet with them and prove your worth. Make this next meeting count. I am placing you in charge for the next four days so you can run the operation this time. It was requested by the directors, so they can get a feel for your style and efficiency. I gladly agreed. I will be staying back at the office and Sari will be going in my place."

"John, you really are the best boss that I have ever had. Thank you so much. How can I return the favor?"

"I am asking a favor of you in return and I hope that you will honor it."

"Absolutely! What do you need from me?"

"If and when they offer you the position on the island project and you get to choose your team, please don't choose me as a team member."

"What??? Why wouldn't you want to work on this project? Do you not agree with it or something?"

"No, nothing like that. Olivia, I'm too old to be traipsing around like that. I want to be home with my wife every night, not gone five or six days at a time, only spending one or two at home with her. It's just not where I am in life. This is your shot to do something meaningful. Make it count, but leave me here where I am happy, please."

"Your wife would miss you like crazy, wouldn't she? What about the rest of the team, though? Are you going to want me to leave some of them behind as well? I realize that it could be hard to replace all of us at one time."

"No, I won't ask that of you. As a group, you all work together so well, complimenting each other's strengths and weaknesses. There are others in the office that would benefit from being able to move up. I have some ideas for competent candidates to fill the holes that you will leave."

"It scares me to talk like this, John. What if I don't succeed? What if I fail miserably and ruin my career?"

Pulling up in front of Claudia's apartment, John replied, "My suggestion to you is to let that go for now and focus on being the team lead for the next four days. That is where your concern needs to be right now. The rest will follow, because none of it will happen if you do not succeed at this. Sitting next to you are the files that you will need. You have a bit of a drive ahead. It should give you enough time to go over all of it and form a plan."

"Yes sir, I will do that. Thank you so much for everything!"

That night at the hotel a slight noise pulled Olivia from her slumber. Not moving a muscle until she could figure out what it was, she listened intently for another sound, opening her eyes slowly. There was a small ray of light coming in through the window at her back, illuminating the entire room in a soft, dim glow. A slight noise came again. Maybe it's just Claudia making sleep sounds, she thought, as she had heard her come in quite some time ago. She looked over toward her bed and saw the sheets move and fall partially away.

Her eyes were filled with two bodies that were so beautiful together, naked, exploring each other, straining toward completion. The need for silence only seemed to intensify the connection between them. Sari's beautiful ebony skin, moving slowly over Claudia's substantial milk white flesh, so quietly, slowly, gently, causing Claudia to arch her back, straining to be closer to the source of pleasure, Sari's lips moving over Claudia's collarbone to her ample breasts, pausing to tease and tempt with hand and mouth, moving lower still, until Sari's head was resting between Claudia's legs, making Claudia whimper ever so softly. They moved silently, only the softest murmurs escaping them in an attempt to not wake Olivia. *Well, that didn't work out so well, now did it*, Olivia thought to herself. She closed her eyes to block out the sight of her friends caught up in overwhelming passion, wondering wistfully whether she would ever be able to feel that again.

14

"You have been oddly quiet since we got back from fieldwork, babe. Are you alright?" Sari asked Olivia with concern. "You are always so lost in thought, or too busy to hang out with any of us."

"I'm fine. I just have a lot on my mind right now with the meeting coming up tomorrow. I need to convince them to let me run the project solo. It's my idea, so it's only right, but they make the calls, so we'll see," she replied, thinking that she should have just driven herself to the airport.

"It is not just that. You haven't hung out with us since we got back. What is going on with you, Liv? I'm worried and so is everyone else. Except John. He never worries. Says that you will come around when you are ready."

"Everyone else as in who?"

"Dave, Tammy, Claudia, and most importantly me, Liv. We all love you and want to help with whatever is going on."

"Sari, I cannot focus on anything but the project right now. Anything else is a waste of my energy. I am going to win them over so they offer me the position that I want. That is my only goal and concern right now."

Olivia looked out the window at the airport coming up on the right, planes coming and going, taking people to destinations, to their future, both bad and good. I wonder what tomorrow will bring. Will it bring joy or sorrow? Will it be the pinnacle of my career, or just another letdown in my life? If I can't have a fully satisfying personal life, then I should, at the very least, be able to have a satisfying professional life. She scowled and chastised herself. I have great friends and a beautiful home with my fur babies, Max and Molly. I just miss being able to be intimate with someone. I don't even need a full-on relationship, just something so that I know that I am not broken forever, that I can still feel and be aroused without anger and betrayal ruining it. Four nights of seeing Sari and Claudia with their bodies entangled, pleasuring each other, should have turned her on mentally or physically, but she'd had no reaction. It was beautiful in the sense that she appreciated the sensuality of it much like how someone appreciated a work of art.

"Earth to Olivia," Sari commented with a sigh. "See, this is what I am talking about. You just drift off and disappear somewhere in that pretty little head."

"Sorry, I was just off thinking about some stuff. Pop the trunk, would you, so I can grab my bag."

"What had you so deep in thought?" Sari asked while grabbing Olivia's arm so she couldn't get away. "I'm not letting go until you tell me, babe. You can't win anyone over for this project if you can't even focus on a small conversation. So, spill it now. Get it out of the way so it isn't a distraction to you."

Tears fill Olivia's eyes. "I am broken. When I watched you with Claudia, pleasuring her over and over, so many times, during those four days of fieldwork I expected it to turn me on. It didn't though. It made me feel nothing except sadness that I likely won't ever get to have that again." Tears spilled down her cheeks. "Are you happy now? Now you know what's wrong." She jerked her arm away and went to grab her bag.

Jumping out of the car, Sari reached for Olivia, pulling her tight so that their bodies were almost one. "I'm so sorry. We tried to be quiet. I didn't think that it would bother you if we had sex. You haven't ever cared who I slept with before."

Muffled against Sari's chest, Olivia said, "I don't care who you have sex with, I don't care that you had sex with Claudia, I don't even care that I ended up seeing it so much. I just don't want to be numb the rest of my life, and I am afraid that is what I will be."

"Maybe you just need to do it. Just bite the bullet and have sex with someone. Maybe that will wake up that desire inside that you are missing. Find someone that is attractive to you and try it."

"I can't even pleasure myself without all of the bullshit flooding my mind. How am I supposed to be with someone else? Listen, I have to go. We'll talk when I get back." Grabbing her bag, she turned. "I don't want to think about anything besides my project until after the meeting." Olivia kissed Sari on the cheek and ran into the airport to catch her flight.

What felt like days later, but was truly only hours, Olivia found herself standing in a conference room in front of the group of people that literally had her career in their hands. She presented them with her ideas including a breakdown of costs, benefits to communities, and how this project could help so many people. Once she had finished, Olivia waited for the questions to come but was instead met with silence. She shifted uncomfortably, not sure what to expect. As she cleared her throat, about to address the room again, Mr. Rhodes, the director of NED, stood.

"We asked you to come here today, Miss Titos, to give us the cost analysis and breakdown of your island project to see if it matches our project budget availability, and it does. We have had many discussions between RED and NED and feel that your idea could indeed be a solution to many of the problems that our communities are faced with every day. However, I and others on the board are still concerned that your previous history with Ink will get in the way of operations and cause this plan to fail. Failure is not an option if we give the go-ahead to move forward with this immense undertaking," Mr. Rhodes stated with an unfeeling expression.

"With all due respect, Mr. Rhodes, my history with Ink is exactly what will make this project more successful than anyone here could imagine," Olivia replied fiercely.

Looking over at the woman to his right, Mr. Rhodes raised his eyebrows as if waiting for her to speak, but she simply nodded her head and gestured for him to continue.

"Strong words spoken do not ensure success, nor do they instill any kind of confidence in your ability to make this endeavor a fruitful one. We cannot build the foundation of the future on your whims and emphatic words."

"With all due respect, Director, this is not a whim, and they are not simply emphatic words. I am willing to stake my entire career on the success of Euphoria."

One of the women on the panel spoke softly. "And what of the careers of your employees should you manage to secure the director position? Are you willing to risk them as well? Because that is indeed what you would be doing, Miss Titos."

Reading the nameplate, Olivia responded, "Ms. Blackborne, I am confident that I can create a place where addicts can be free of judgement and the general public can feel comfortable knowing that they have safe streets once again. It may not be perfect, but it will make an impact that none will be able to deny."

Rhodes cut in, speaking gruffly with disdain evident in his voice. "You continue to talk a good game, but you have brought no proof to support your statements. Are we supposed to put taxpayer money on the line just because you feel strongly about this project?"

"I am not sure how else to convince you that I am the only correct choice for the director position of Euphoria. I have the experience and the ambition to make this island project a success for both the RED and the NED. Never have the two agencies come together to work on a project like this one. With me as the face of the project, an RED employee, the NED has a certain safety net as I am not previously affiliated with the Directive. Therefore, if I fail, which I will not do, Mr. Rhodes, you and the NED will have clean hands. I believe that those that represent the RED here have full confidence in my ability to create a space that is efficient and effective."

The soft-spoken woman stood, addressing Olivia gently. "Miss Titos, we have much to discuss at this time so if you could, please see yourself out to the lounge so that we may do so. We will send for you when you are required."

Olivia sat in the lounge for what seemed to be an eternity, time dragging on torturously, the clock's hands never seeming to move before she saw movement in the hall. She sat up straight as a young man entered, expecting him to call her back to the boardroom. Disappointment was palpable on her face as he made his way to the coffee machine. The frown was still on her striking face when she heard a low laugh and her name being spoken. Embarrassment raced through her body as she tried her best to make her face unreadable.

The woman motioned toward the door, smiling at Olivia's discomfort. "Right this way please."

The click of her heels on the marble floors gave Olivia some confidence back as she made her way back into the oppressive boardroom. She kept her feelings well masked as she sat before the board again, awaiting their decision.

Ms. Blackborne spoke first. "It is the opinion of this council that because you did conceive this idea that you should be the one to take the lead on the running of the island once the building has been completed. You will move from your current position into a director's position once you have completed all the required trainings and testing. You will be responsible for the hiring of the staff for the island as well as being tasked with the day-to-day operations. This means that you, as well as your staff, will be residing on the island for extended periods of time. There is no way to make daily transport cost-effective."

Olivia nodded, stunned into silence by the offer of a director's position and the reality that her dream was coming true.

Before she could speak Mr. Rhodes stood, his face looking disgruntled. "While you may have secured the majority of the votes, Miss Titos, do not think that it was unanimous by any means. There are those of us that feel that you will fail miserably, but the choice was not ours alone to make. I for one vehemently fought against you being appointed. Know that I will personally be watching you and this project very closely!"

"I welcome the observation and guidance that I am sure you will offer to the project, Mr. Rhodes," Olivia replied sweetly.

For a fleeting moment she felt a tightness in her stomach, a warning of being careful of what you wish for, but it passed and was forgotten in mere seconds, though it may have been a good idea to ponder that feeling a bit more.

15

After the intensity of the day before, Olivia sat quietly in her kitchen enjoying the tantalizing scent of her steaming mug of coffee. She thoroughly enjoyed the solitude of her life and was slightly concerned that she would miss that once she began her new career as a director. On the island she would be around people and be responsible for them all the time. It was exciting, but also a burden that she would have to carry on her shoulders. She sipped on the hot coffee and remembered that she had sent Joe a text very late last night. When she checked her texts she smiled, seeing that she had a message waiting for her.

Why don't you swing by the shelter this morning so we can chat about Molly's predicament?

The tingle of anticipation sang in her body for a brief moment, and she quickly replied, *See you soon*, before she talked herself out of it.

Driving through the busy streets, Olivia found herself looking forward to seeing Joe at the shelter. She had decided to bring some donations along to help the shelter kitties in any way that she could. In the passenger seat of her car was a box full of brand-new toys, wet cat food, and a tub of kitty litter. These cats had tugged at her heart, and she wanted to save them all, but knew that wasn't possible. She was going to have enough kitties in her home with Max, Molly, and the new kittens, whenever they arrived, so this was the best she could do for them. She had already set up a monthly donation that was coming directly out of her paycheck and going to the shelter. Every little bit counts, she thought, smiling in anticipation of the playtime with the cats, and if she were being honest, the thought of hanging out with Joe was aiding that smile on her face.

Pulling into the parking lot, Olivia checked her reflection in the rearview mirror, shrugged, and got out to grab the items on the other side of the car. Considering how hot it already was that early in the morning, she had decided to wear jean shorts and a teal cotton tank top, but was now questioning that idea, cats' claws and all. With a shrug she slammed the car door shut with her hip and made her way to the front door of the shelter.

Joe was already there, holding the door open for her and taking many of the items from her to carry them to the counter. He had the same khaki uniform, same dust-colored hair, and the same friendly smile as the last time she'd seen him, all of which put Olivia instantly at ease. He opened the door to the back, letting Olivia go ahead of him, then taking the lead as they headed to the storage room to put the donations away before heading to the play area.

The storage was more like a large walk-in closet, Olivia noticed, not really a full-sized room, with shelving on each wall. The colors were dark grays and dark greens, giving the room an almost depressing feel, along with the lack of needed items on the shelves. Sure, they had food and litter, some toys, towels, and blankets, but there was room for so much more. A sadness came over Olivia as she began to truly under-stand the reality of how the shelter ran and how difficult it must be to work there. Everyone was doing the best they could to provide for these animals, knowing that some of them may never find a home. Placing the new toys on the shelf and trailing a hand across them, she asked softly, "What happens to the cats and dogs that don't get adopted?"

"If we can't get them adopted or find a foster home for them they usually just stay here. We are a no-kill shelter. It just means that we can't take any new animals in once we are full, and we are always full of cats. We only have two dogs right now, but a couple of my cowork-ers take them home on the weekends. Fostering helps them socialize with kids and other animals. It helps to get them adopted faster when they have exposure to those things."

"So, some shelters euthanize them?"

"Unfortunately, yes, after a certain period of time, they do. I wish more people would understand the importance of spaying and neutering their pets."

"I cannot even imagine having to choose which animal gets put to sleep. It's heartbreaking to even think about."

"I am glad that our policy does not include euthanizing animals, unless of course it is the humane thing to do. We had a dog tied to our back door one time that was filled with cancerous tumors. Poor pup was in so much pain, it was the right thing to do in that case."

"That must have been hard to see. Why did the owners drop him off like that?"

"I really don't know. They just tied him to the back door and left him there. His last couple of days, he was spoiled and loved, though. We all made sure of that. Speaking of spoiled, how is Molly fitting into your household?"

"Max is completely in love with her and so am I. She is the sweetest thing. I wonder how Max will react when the kittens arrive."

"Will you be sending the kittens back here when they are weaned from Molly?"

"What? No way! Why would I do that?"

"You adopted one cat, not all of her kittens. We would take them and find homes for them if you wanted us to."

"Absolutely not! Max and Molly will be very unhappy if I take away their babies. I have enough room for all of them. Molly will be getting spayed as soon as possible after she gives birth. I've already spoken with my veterinarian."

"You are an amazing woman, Olivia. I am sure those cats will have the best home they could ever hope for."

"I do hope I can provide that for them. Can we go play with the cats now, please?"

"For sure! Wait until you see the cat that we got in once Molly left and opened up a space!"

Walking back down the hallway to the playroom, Olivia watched the way Joe walked with such relaxed confidence, completely at home in his job and comfortable talking to whoever happened to come in the door. He seemed like a genuinely good person that cared about the animals and finding their perfect match. He certainly had with Molly. She was the perfect fit for both Olivia and Max.

Turning the corner while still lost in thought, Olivia slammed into the back of Joe, who had stopped in front of the playroom door, causing both of them to fall forward. Joe managed to steady himself quickly, reaching out for Olivia as she fell toward the concrete floor. He managed to scoop her up in his arms before contact. Face-to-face and breathless, they stared into each other's eyes, Joe's arms wrapped securely around Olivia's waist, her arms around his neck, both stunned and unsure of what to do next. Joe's eyes flickered closed as he drew a deep breath, and Olivia's gut clenched, butterflies erupting like hot magma from a volcano as she braced for his kiss, wondering how his lips would feel on hers and what he would taste like.

Shifting back to a standing position and setting her firmly on her own feet, Joe opened his eyes and gently brushed the hair out of Olivia's face, staring into her eyes for another moment before releasing her to stand on her own. Completely confused as to what had just happened, she watched Joe open the door to the playroom and walk inside. He looked back, asking, "Are you alright?"

"Yes, sorry. I was just a bit shaken up. I didn't mean to almost knock us over. Thank you for catching me."

"It was my pleasure, Olivia," Joe commented sensually.

The tone in his voice caused more confusion in her mind, her thoughts running around like chaotic school children just released for summer break. She wondered why he hadn't tried to kiss her. Was he not attracted to her? Did he not like women? Was there something wrong with her? Why did she even care anyway?

A sudden epiphany hit her like a ton of bricks, knocking the wind out of her. She had reacted to him in a way that she hadn't reacted to anybody in over two years. She had wanted him to kiss her. She had wanted to feel that heat. She could even feel the physical effect that his intense gaze had caused within her body.

Well goddamn it. That was exciting by itself, but she still didn't understand why he hadn't made a move to close the space between them.

Instead of continuing to dwell, she moved into the room, waiting for him to select the cats that needed time out of their cages today.

Bringing in four relatively young cats, he told her individual stories of how they came to be here at the shelter. "You see this calico here? Her name is Colors. She moved into Molly's old place. It's a good thing we got to her in time. She was severely malnourished and dehydrated. She wouldn't have lasted much longer without care. We got a call about a cat stuck in a dumpster next to an abandoned building. We aren't sure if someone threw her in there or if she somehow managed to get in there on her own. She is doing very well now, and I imagine that she will be adopted quickly once she's listed. People seem to love calico cats."

"I can see why they would. She is beautiful."

"She is also cuddly and playful, a couple of particularly important qualities that will also attract potential owners."

Rolling balls with bells, flicking feathers attached to a long string on a stick, playing with laser pointers, scratching backs, and just giving love and attention to as many cats as possible was the goal for the rest of the day. Olivia stayed in the playroom with the cats all day, Joe switching them out every now and again so they could all get some time to stretch their legs or just bask in the sun shining through the window. Joe had to attend to customers a few times, leaving Olivia alone with the cats, content to be there, hoping that she was making a difference for them, adding some love to their lives.

She was happily sitting on the floor with a couple of senior cats when Joe came back in. They weren't as playful, but they did love lounging and having their ears rubbed. An old toothless tiger cat had made himself comfortable, curling up in her lap as she sat cross-legged on the area rug. She was stroking his face, telling him how pretty and sweet he was, when she heard a sound and looked up. Joe was watching her from the doorway, a strange look in his eyes, one that he quickly blinked away when he noticed that she had seen him. Smiling and walking into the room, he said, "I'm going to have to borrow this room for a bit. I have a prospective couple here looking for their first cat."

"Oh, no problem. I should get going anyway. I've already been here most of the day. I'm sure you will be closing up after they leave anyway. It's getting late."

"I wouldn't say that it's late. It's only four o'clock in the afternoon, but we do close at five o'clock on Sundays, so yeah, I will be."

"Thank you so much for today. It was nice to just relax and play with the cats."

"It's not a problem at all. Here, let me walk you to the back door. That entrance is closer to your car. I can make sure you get there safely and then go back to the front."

Walking down the hallway to the back of the building, Olivia felt a twinge of sadness at leaving the shelter, where things were so simple and yet, so complicated. It was a good day, a relaxing day, for her and for the cats. Every one of the cats was able to get out and have playroom time. It made her feel good about herself to do something good for someone else; well, something else. As they reached the door, Olivia smiled up at Joe, glowing with happiness. "Thank you again for letting me come down today. I had such a good time. One of the best days I've had in a while, honestly."

That strange look came back to Joe's eyes, intense and confusing, his arm coming around her waist. "I should have done this earlier." He leaned in and fit his mouth to hers, kissing her lightly, his tongue drawing lazy circles on her lips, pulling a moan from her, but not moving at all to deepen the kiss. He let her set the pace. She had to decide how deep they were going to go, if at all. His patience playing on her mouth was making her mind buzz.

She questioned her sanity as she leaned in slightly, opening her lips and allowing his tongue to enter, dancing with hers as her arms wrapped around his neck with a mind of their own. His hands gripped her hips firmly, holding her to him. She moaned softly, her body reacting, feeling a fire start to flicker inside, until she was transported again to that dark place, eyes seeing what her mind did not want to comprehend, the pain, the betrayal, the end of her life as she knew it. The tiny flame was fanned out with those intrusive thoughts, but it had been there.

Pulling back slowly so as not to alarm Joe and make him think that he did anything wrong, breathless and flushed, she placed a hand on his face, smiled, and turned to walk out the door. "Wait," he said. Pulling her back into his arms, fingers under her chin, he tipped her head up slightly, lowering his mouth to hers again and kissing her so softly, so seductively, that her mind went completely blank. All she could do was feel. With his mouth hovering above hers, he whispered, "Go to dinner with me. Please. Next Friday evening. I can pick you up."

Still dazed and unsteady on her feet, she replied quietly, "Okay. I'll call you."

He smiled and leaned in again, kissing her slowly and thoroughly. As he pulled away breathless, he whispered, "You should go, I'm having a hard time keeping my hands off you. I will watch from here to make sure you get to your car safely."

Not knowing what to say at that point, Olivia nodded, still in shock at her reaction. She walked to her car, sliding in before she saw Joe close the door to the shelter while smiling and waving. Sitting there in the parking lot, she sat in stunned silence, going over everything that had happened in her mind.

16

The heat wave that week had left everyone in the city miserable, sweat-soaked, and seeking out air-conditioned establishments wherever they could. The air-conditioning unit in the office had stopped working and couldn't be fixed until the parts came in the following week, so Olivia had improvised and scheduled her interviews for potential team members to meet at Jcb's, which still had running air. It may have been a bar and grill, but it was blissfully cool inside, making it much more comfortable to meet with people. Besides, if they got upset about meeting at a bar and grill, then they weren't the right fit for her team anyway.

Tammy wandered over to her table after the gentleman that Olivia had been interviewing walked out the door. "He seemed really nice. Do you need a refill on your drink or something to eat? You've been at this for almost three hours now."

"No, thank you. I might grab a bite after this next interview, though. She's my last one for the day," Olivia replied, wondering if the next interviewee would cause issues among the team.

"Alright, but if you need anything, just flag me down, darling. Look who just walked in. My Ameera. Oh man she makes my insides flutter. I wonder what she's doing here?" Rushing over to the woman happily, Tammy gushed, "You look so professional and office-like today. Such a sexy look on you! What brings you in today, love? I'm not forgetting plans, am I?"

"No, sweetness, I am here for an interview with a woman named Olivia."

"Oh man! You're her last interview?"

Shrugging dismissively, Ameera said, "Yes, I would assume so. Bring me to her."

Looking uncomfortable and glancing at Ameera, Tammy led her over to the corner table that Olivia was occupying. "Your uh, your final interview is here, Olivia."

Olivia looked up to see Ameera and motioned for her to sit down across from her, moving into professional mode. "Hello Ameera, how are you today?"

"I'm well, Olivia, thank you for asking. How are you?"

"Very well, thank you. I see that you are here to apply for the health and nutrition supervisor position. You're aware that this project requires you to be away from home for extended periods of time, correct?"

"Yes, I was aware of that when I applied for the position. I have nothing tying me down here that would keep me from such an amazing opportunity. I am passionate about helping those addicted to drugs as I had my own encounters with Ink," Ameera's face was serious and unemotional.

Olivia asked questions, going over all the protocols and possible scenarios and answering all the questions that Ameera had about the project. The interview lasted well beyond the time of the others, and it was purely professional but intense in the depth of the discussion, from how the island idea came to be to the approval process through the RED and NED and to the timeline for the island program.

Olivia was pleased with Ameera's responses and her professionalism, as well as the qualifications that she could bring to the table. However, the issue was, could they all work together in a professional manner? Especially Dave and Ameera, considering the intimate relationship that he and Tammy had with her. She wasn't really worried about Sari. The composure and emotional detachedness that was Sari's way would allow for her and Ameera to work together with no problems. Stress settled in as Olivia contemplated all she had to think about in such a short time. Her top picks for her supervisory positions needed to be in by Sunday evening, which was only two days away.

Olivia pondered how to best broach the subject. Finally deciding that being straightforward was best, she asked, "How do you propose to traverse the fine line of professionalism and your personal life considering your relationships with both Dave and Sari?"

"My personal life has no impact on my professional life. My career is the single most important thing to me. Relationships are enjoyable but they're not what sustains me."

"So, you don't feel that your connection with either of them will create any conflicts on the island? We'll all be working close together for extended periods of time."

Ameera looked Olivia directly in the eye. "I would cut off any relationship that got in the way of my career trajectory. Nothing, and I mean nothing, is as important to me as my career."

A little surprised at the vehemence in Ameera when speaking of her career, Olivia considered that everyone had their own life story and reasons for the paths that they chose.

"Thank you for your time, Ameera. It was a pleasure. I'll let you know either way next week."

"Thank you for the opportunity. I think that I would be a great fit. Now that the interview is over, would you like to get something to eat? To be honest with you, I was a little nervous, so I skipped lunch today, and now I'm starving. Though I do understand if you wish to decline the invitation as my potential future employer. Please know that I am not trying to get in your good graces. The interview and dinner would be two separate occurrences in my book."

Mulling it over in her mind and feeling her stomach gnawing at her from lack of food, Olivia smiled, saying, "Sure. Let's grab dinner. I'm starving as well. They have some of the best food in the city here."

"Sari has brought me here before and I had the wings. They were to die for. I haven't come here since because it's a bit far for me to drive and I like to have a drink with dinner occasionally. Besides, Tammy works here, so it can be a bit awkward if I have a friend with me."

"I can see why you would want to avoid that. She is sweet, but quite boisterous at times."

"She is a lot of fun and so is Dave, but I'm not into settling down and making promises to people. I watched my brother commit to a woman that he loved, get married, buy a house, start talking about having babies, and then one day she was gone. She left him for another man that ended up knocking her and another woman up at the same time and disappearing off the face of the earth."

"Wow, that's awful! I don't even know what to say."

"Broke his heart. I swore I would never let anything like that happen to me. My career fulfills me. I have no need to settle down."

Flagging Tammy down so they could order drinks and food from the kitchen, Olivia just shook her head. "I don't know how some people can be so irresponsible, especially with another person's life."

"That's not even the worst of it. So, she reaches out to my brother, begging him to take her back because she's scared and alone, pregnant with no one to help her, and he agrees. He just scoops her up and brings her back home like nothing ever happened. And now he is raising another man's child, and she is as unstable as ever, always wanting to bring this person home or that person home. I mean, if that's how he wants to live, it is his choice. It's the only way she says she'll stay, but come on, now you have a child to care for. All of that playing around should be put aside until the child is grown."

Tammy approached the table with a questioning look. "Can I get you something?" she asked, seeming surprised that they were both still there after the interview should have concluded.

Olivia smiled. "Yes, we would like to place an order. Pizza and hot wings. I will have whiskey on the rocks, and whatever drink she would like. You can put it all on my bill."

Arching her eyebrow, but not questioning it, Tammy turned to Ameera, waiting for her drink order. "I'll have a margarita please."

"I'll get that right in. Be right back with your drinks."

Going back to chatting with each other, Olivia said, "I've never been one to have more than one partner. I feel like it complicates things way too much. Having one is challenging enough."

Tammy arrived with their food a short time later, the spicy smell of hot wings wafting through the air and making their mouths water in anticipation. Walking away, Tammy looked back over her shoulder, an envious look on her pretty face, and her full lips forming a slight frown.

Digging into the food in front of them, the women continued their conversation, eating and laughing, the beginnings of an unlikely friendship forming over greasy hot wings and the cheesy perfection of pizza. The possibility of ordering dessert became the next hot topic. They were so immersed in tantalizing images of lava cake and warm chocolate chip cookie bars with vanilla ice cream that they didn't notice Sari and Dave had walked in.

"Well well well, what do we have here," Sari joked loud enough to cause both Olivia and Ameera to jump out of their skins. Laughter rang through the air. "Score one for making Ameera jump. She is usually cool as a cucumber."

Dave laughed. "You've got that right. I haven't found anything that fazes her yet."

Glaring at them, Ameera said coolly, "Neither of you has the mental capacity to come up with something intelligent enough to faze me. I've seen it or been through it all, my pets."

Suddenly unsure of themselves, realizing that they never had the upper hand in the face of Ameera's cool dismissal, they stood awkwardly, wondering if they should sit with Ameera and Olivia or go find a seat at the bar. Staring at them stonily for a bit longer, Ameera let them stew in their discomfort, waiting until the moment they were about to walk away, and then she asked sweetly, "Aren't you going to sit with us?" her voice dripping with honey and temptation.

Sitting beside Olivia, Sari said, "You interviewed for a position with Olivia, didn't you? I knew you were qualified, but I wasn't sure if you would put yourself in that position with your history."

"My history is my own, Sari. Don't make me regret sharing my secrets."

Both Dave and Olivia looked on curiously, wondering what secrets she could have that would make applying for a position on the island surprising.

Olivia, having plenty of patience, opted to wait it out and didn't ask, knowing that if Ameera genuinely wanted the job, she would come clean with her sooner rather than later.

"Olivia, I know you can't tell me right now, but I really want to be on your team," Ameera said sincerely, reaching for her hand and squeezing it tight. "You have such passion in you for this project, only good can come of it. I'll work to help you achieve your dream if I'm chosen."

Dave looked between Olivia and Ameera, not saying anything, but likely realizing that if Ameera got hired, they would all be on the island together, living and working there.

As if sensing his train of thought, Sari said, "You can't let these stray thoughts determine your future, man. You have figured out what's right for you. If you don't think you can handle the island, then you need to let Liv know now. It's totally cool if you want to stay here with Tammy. I just hope that if you do, she commits."

"Don't let what we do be a deciding factor for you, Dave," Ameera stated very matter-of-factly. "I will always choose my career over a person. What we do is fun, but it's not something that will last forever. It will only last as long as it suits me. Which it does right now, but maybe not tomorrow." She glanced toward the bar and saw Tammy shooting daggers of jealousy toward the table.

"Worry about yourself instead of these women Dave," Sari jeered.

"Sari, you're so compassionate sometimes," Olivia laughed, shaking her head.

"Don't inflate Sari's ego so much, Olivia, it won't fit out the door when she leaves," Ameera joked. "Speaking of leaving, I need to head out. It was a pleasure spending time with you today, Olivia. I truly hope to hear from you soon on the position, or if you just want to get together and have a drink." She waved goodbye to everyone, purposefully ignoring Tammy on the way out. "Dave, walk me to my car."

"She can be a cold one, can't she?" Olivia asked Sari.

"Yes, she can. She doesn't make emotional attachments to anybody, always protecting herself above all else. She would be an asset to you professionally. Her career is the one thing that she cares about."

"I have some tough decisions to make this weekend for sure with three open positions, and now Dave seems unsure of joining the team. I just need to trust that it will all come together. Then if Dave is still on board I'll have to wonder if there will be some sort of issue because of what is going on here if I hire Ameera. She is incredibly qualified for the position though and would be my top candidate otherwise," Olivia replied, knowing that she was going to hire her, just not ready to say it out loud.

"Liv, everything will fall into place for you. I promise I will help make your vision a reality. But... shouldn't you be worrying about your date tomorrow night instead of work?"

"Oh my god, Sari, I'm half-excited and half-terrified."

"At least you feel something Liv. That's a start."

17

Sari's words rolled through Olivia's mind as she sifted through the clothes in her closet. She may be feeling some sort of way about her date tonight, but it wasn't the same as having sexual urges. Who knows, maybe she would be inundated with desire and be rolling around on her cushy king-sized bed with a super-hot guy before the clock struck midnight.

Olivia laughed at herself as she continued to paw through her clothes trying to find something that said I'm sexy but maybe not too available. She wasn't one for quick sex, but it had happened once or twice. She fingered a soft cotton dress that fell to mid-thigh and draped on her body like a drunken lover as her thoughts began to drift back to one of those nights. Specifically, the night she had met Aria.

A light brush of fur along her bare leg sent a quick shiver through her body, pulling her from what would have been a disastrous trip down memory lane. Olivia watched as Molly made her way into the darkness of the oversized closet. A bit confused, Olivia peered deep into the corner to see what Molly was up to. The cats didn't normally go in her closet as they preferred the guest bedroom since it was rarely used. She couldn't see where Molly had gone so she turned the light on and opened the doors fully. She could just barely see the fluff of Molly's long black tail sticking out from behind a stack of shoe boxes. Calling to her softly, Olivia began to move items out of the way so she could further investigate her cat's odd behavior.

A small gasp escaped Olivia as she finally understood what Molly was doing in her closet. She had pulled some of her softest throw blankets in the far corner behind the boxes and had made a nest of sorts.

Oh my gosh, it must almost be time for her to have the kittens! Olivia backed out of the closet but didn't replace the boxes. She wanted to be able to keep an eye on the cats. A soft meow came from behind her as Max made his way to Molly's side. Her heart swelled with love and worry for her cats. She had no idea what to do for them if Molly was in labor. Molly didn't seem to be uncomfortable, but Olivia didn't want to take chances.

She reached for her phone with a sigh—so much for my date tonight —and sent Joe a text explaining the situation and asking for his advice.

His reply was almost immediate and made her smile. I can come over and take a look at her if you want. If she's in labor we can eat in. I can even do the cooking.

Sounds good to me. I have all the ingredients for spaghetti and meatballs, that is if you like it. Not sure who, but I hear some people don't like Italian.

Haha that's funny. Spaghetti sounds great if we can't go out. See you in about an hour.

She sent him the address and looked around at the disaster she had created while trying to find something to wear. She grabbed the pile of clothes from her bed and made her way to the guest room to hang the clothes in the other closet. She didn't want to disturb Molly, so she pulled the mid-length sundress from the pile instead of continuing the search for the perfect outfit.

She looked at the antique clock that hung on the wall, one of her grandmother's gifts to her upon the woman's passing, and saw that she only had another forty minutes until Joe was supposed to arrive. With a rushed groan she hurried to the bathroom for a quick shower and sent a prayer up that he wouldn't get there before she finished getting ready.

Her hair was still wet, and she was just putting the finishing touches on her make-up when she heard the doorbell. A nervous flutter danced in her belly as she walked across the plush carpet to the front door. As she turned the handle to open the door a quick feeling of panic shot through her chest and made her breath hitch. *What am I thinking? I'm so not ready to be on a date with anyone, especially if we stay in for it.*

"You look beautiful, Olivia!"

A slight blush rose in her cheeks. "Thank you. You look very handsome," she said, her eyes taking in the khakis and black polo shirt that fit his sculpted body very well. Clearing her suddenly parched throat, she said, "Please, come in."

"You have a lovely home," Joe commented as he looked around the living room, noting the oversized couch with luxurious pillows and throw blankets. He nodded toward the paintings hanging on the wall, whistling softly. "Those are impressive. I've seen some like them in a gallery downtown."

"Yes, a woman from a small community near the central forests painted many before she passed. It was tragic really. I met her at an exhibition. She was lovely."

"Do you know what happened to her?"

"She was thrown from a cliff by her ex-husband because he was hoping to steal her land. It was a big story closer to where she lived. I only know so much because my ex was a journalist and she chased what she liked to call the epic stories."

"Well, that sounds pretty epic to me. You did say 'she' when referring to your ex, right?" Joe asked with a hint of confusion.

Sighing quietly before answering, Olivia internally questioned why she'd even mentioned her ex. "Yes. I am bisexual. And before you ask, I'm attracted to both men and women equally."

A bit flustered and embarrassed, Joe responded quickly. "Oh! That's cool. I hope I didn't make you uncomfortable with that question."

"You're fine. Follow me if you want to check on Molly for me. She's um, well, she's in my bedroom closet."

"Perfect excuse to get me in your bedroom," Joe teased.

Shooting a serious side-eye at him, Olivia gestured toward the hall. "I'm sorry, seriously. Just kidding. Please, lead the way."

They could hear a small mew coming from the closet as they entered the bedroom. Olivia moved to check on Molly, but Joe was faster and reached the opening first. A slight feeling of irritation ran through Olivia as she watched him take point. She wasn't used to sharing her space or stepping aside and letting someone else take the lead. *He's just trying to be helpful. Relax. He knows better than I do in this instance.*

"She is doing just fine, Olivia. Come look," Joe said softly, motioning for her to take a peek at Molly.

She moved to the closet and leaned in, seeing her cat was comfortable and seeming to be doing alright with labor.

Joe motioned again, this time toward the door. "Let's go cook some dinner and give her some privacy."

A short time later meatballs had been made and were simmering in a hearty red sauce that Joe had doctored to taste. He scooped a small portion onto a spoon and held it to Olivia's lips. "Make sure to blow," he said, the underlying sexual implication evident in his tone, "it's hot."

Arching a well-manicured eyebrow at him, she blew on the sauce and carefully took the spoon into her mouth. "Oh my," she exclaimed, "this is delicious!"

"I know how to make it good," he said, a smirk playing across his mouth. "Just wait and see."

Trying to ignore the innuendo, Olivia began prepping the green salad, an uncomfortable feeling beginning to settle in the pit of her stomach. This was not a simple dinner out, not a simple first date. There was a man in her home, her sanctuary. A man that she had thought was soft and sweet because of how he cared for the animals at the shelter. But it dawned on her now that she did not know this man at all. From the sexual comments and gestures to the expectation that she should enjoy all of it, here in her kitchen Joe seemed to have become like every toxic man that she had ever known in her life. She had dealt with this often enough before to see where it was headed. Disappointment began to settle in, though Olivia did her best to shake it off, to give the "date" another shot.

"Salad is done. How is everything on the stove?" Olivia asked quietly.

"About five minutes and it will be ready to plate if you want to get the dishes ready."

"Perfect. I'm going to go check on Molly quickly. Be right back."

In her bedroom Olivia looked in on Molly, and seeing that everything was quiet, she took a few minutes for herself to just breathe. Maybe this is just his way when he is nervous. Maybe he isn't sure how to react to being in my home. Or maybe he is just like most men, sex-hungry and looking for a woman to get between the sheets. Shaking her head to clear her thoughts, she composed herself and headed back to the kitchen.

"I was about to come looking for you. I thought maybe it was a subtle invitation back to your bedroom."

Ignoring the comment, Olivia asked, "Are we ready to eat?"

Making a grand sweeping gesture with his hands toward the kitchen island, he said, "Dinner is served, my lady."

Hoping for an uneventful but pleasant meal, Olivia sat and began to dish the fragrant food onto plates. She began to relax as the meal progressed, small talk was made, and everything seemed to be going in a positive direction finally.

Joe offered to check on Molly while Olivia cleaned up the island and started doing the dishes. Okay, maybe I judged him a little too harshly. He seems like the guy that I thought I was getting to know. She was looking out the window after loading the last of the dishes when Joe came back into the room.

She turned to speak to him, not realizing how close he was, and they ended up face-to-face. Taking advantage of the situation, Joe wrapped his arms around Olivia, one winding its way up around her shoulders, hand lightly fisted in her hair, the other moving lower around her waist, his hand grabbing and squeezing her behind to pull her close. She could feel his growing manhood pressing against her body. She opened her mouth to protest and was met with his lips closing on hers, his tongue sweeping into her open mouth. Olivia tried to grasp how thoroughly she was being manhandled within sixty seconds as the panic started to build. She shoved against his chest, hard, as anger accompanied by fear tore through her. He stumbled back looking confused, still reaching for her.

"You need to leave. Now!"

"Wait, Olivia, what did I do wrong?"

"Seriously? Just go, Joe. Please."

He nodded and turned to leave, looking back once with a hopeful glance, but was met with a steely gaze. As the door shut Olivia locked it with shaking hands, the adrenaline ripping through her body at a dizzying rate.

She began to cry, sinking to the floor, knees curled to her chest, fearing that she was destined to be alone forever.

18

Olivia could barely contain her excitement as she finalized the setup for the dinner she was hosting. She was thankful that at least one area of her life was heading in the right direction. Olivia couldn't wait for her guests to arrive so she could see the group dynamic and how they interacted with one another. She would also be watching for personality issues that may cause complications. This was the first step of the island project. Her chest swelled with pride knowing that it was going to be an incredible journey to undertake and knowing that it was going to help so many people.

Her doorbell chimed ten minutes before the set arrival time, pleasing Olivia with her team's promptness. She opened the door for Gail, a middle-aged woman with short blonde hair and an infectious laugh, and Dave as well. Seeing Sari's Camaro pulling up, Olivia walked back to the door after showing the others to the living room. Sari and Claudia made their way up to the front door, laughing together as Ameera pulled into the driveway in a sleek black Jaguar. She was followed by a smoke gray jeep driven by Ezekiel, who preferred being called Zek. She was impressed with the promptness of her crew, all arriving ahead of schedule. She led the way into the living room to make introductions. Dave and Gail had already introduced themselves and were animatedly discussing the merits of community housing compared to separate housing on the island. Everyone drifted into small, comfortable conversation groups, and she excused herself to check on the food, getting the go-ahead to seat everyone.

Calling the group to the dining room, each person found their place and sat, the conversation continuing as the servers came around to fill water glasses, asking if anyone would like white or red wine with dinner. Wine glasses were filled, dinner was served, and conversation seemed to flow so well between the people at the table. Olivia finally felt contented that she had chosen her crew well, seeing how well they all connected.

Once the three-course meal was complete, the servers cleared the table, and the cake was brought in. It was made in the shape of an island, covered with sand, palm trees, seashells, and a welcome sign. The sight of it made everyone cheer happily as Olivia called them to attention with the chiming of a utensil on her wine glass.

"I asked all of you here today as an icebreaker, a chance for everyone to meet before we head to the island and see each other day in and day out. Once we arrive, we will be there for extended periods of time, and more so the closer we get to the opening of the island. All of you have been offered positions as supervisors in your areas, with the exception of Claudia who will be working under Dave. I expect great things from all of you. This is our chance, our opportunity, to make an impact on the safety and cleanliness of our region. I have a wonderful feeling about our group. I know that we will be able to accomplish great things together. Enjoy tonight, get to know one another, and celebrate," she said, raising a glass high. "Cheers!"

"Cheers!" the group replied in unison, raising their glasses.

Olivia cut into the beautiful cake, placing pieces on plates for the servers to hand out. There were generous portions for everyone. She told the servers to grab pieces for themselves when they took it back to the kitchen, not wanting leftovers just sitting in the house. Ameera leaned over, having been placed on Olivia's left, and congratulated her on a job well done of choosing her supervisors.

"You really nailed it picking the people that you did. I want to thank you for giving me a chance, knowing that I had my own struggle with Ink years ago."

"You fought that battle and won, Ameera. I respect you for that. I have complete confidence in you and your ability to make sure that residents on the island have access to proper health and nutrition."

"I will do my best to make sure residents are cared for, and I have some ideas on team building when we get to that phase in the plan."

"I know that you will," Olivia said, smiling at Ameera before standing to move the party to another room so that the catering service could clean up and head out. "Shall we move to the patio?" she asked, heading to the back door to lead them outside. Again, each of them split into small groups, discussing important matters about the island or things that they themselves were passionate about. A warm feeling enveloped Olivia, pleased by the scene. They spent another hour or so sitting and talking before people began to say their goodbyes, heading to their own homes for the night. Olivia watched, amused as Ameera beckoned Dave to her side, leaning in and whispering something that made Dave blush and try to hide his face, nodding quickly at her words. She waved goodbye to everyone and walked through the back gate, followed by Zek. Claudia came up to Sari and Olivia, saying that Gail lived close to her, so she would be catching a ride with her. She thanked Olivia for the wonderful evening and for including her, even though Olivia didn't have to. Soon, it was just Sari, Dave, and Olivia sitting by the pool, a bottle of whiskey passing between them.

Dave shook his head no as the bottle came back around, making Sari laugh and say, "Ameera is still punishing Tammy for that shit at the bar the other night, huh?"

"You guys have no idea," Dave said. "She can be cruel when she feels that her authority in certain situations has been questioned."

Olivia's curiosity perked up. "So why did she make you walk her to the car that night?"

"I'm not sure I should tell you. It's personal."

Sari whacked him on the arm. "Dude, we are all friends here, come on."

Dave shrugged and looked away awkwardly, his hesitancy to say anything palpable in his body language. "She told me to get in the car and then she went down on me. She said that I had to tell Tammy all about it and that until she knocked her shit off, that's how it was going to be. I told you she can be bad."

"Oh my goodness, Dave! And you did it? Seriously? What did Tammy do?" Olivia asked incredulously.

"She was pissed and then she cried, and then she apologized like she had done something wrong. I felt so awful about it, but it's like Ameera has this spell over both of us. I don't even know what to do half of the time. Tonight she said to meet her down at the bar when Tammy gets off work, so she can teach her a final lesson and see if she can behave. It's so fucked up, man!"

"If you don't want to participate, you can say no. You have a voice, and you have a choice," Sari stated clearly.

"I know, but she is so tempting, and I did offer to stop all of this for Tammy, but she said no, she still wants to keep doing what we're doing. I think she wants to please Ameera more than I do."

Olivia wondered, "Does she realize that both you and Ameera are going to be working on the island soon? Not that I expect these shenanigans to be happening there, because that is work and you better not screw up."

"Yes, she knows, and she knows that we won't be engaging in any extracurricular activities there."

"Mm-hmm, sure you won't," Sari sarcastically replied.

"Believe what you want, but I have to go meet them. Later, guys. Wish me luck. I swear those two women are going to be the death of me."

Olivia and Sari waved him off, shaking their heads at the situation that he had managed to get himself into. Two headstrong women that apparently loved a challenge, and loved to challenge each other in ridiculous ways, using Dave as their plaything.

"Do you think he knows that this won't end well for him?" Olivia asked Sari.

"Nah, I don't think he has a clue. I feel kind of bad for him. He just wants a house with a white picket fence and the love of a good woman. Neither of those women that he's lying with can or will give that to him."

"Should we warn him then?"

"What good is it going to do? We tried to explain it. I already warned him about Ameera before all of this started, and he jumped in headfirst. I bet he's in love with both of them. Man, it's going to mess him up bad when they both wander off in another direction."

"For his sake, I hope that none of those things happen and that he ends up being the one to call an end to all of it and walk away. I doubt either of the women would bat an eye at that, well maybe Tammy, but for sure not Ameera."

"Speaking of sex, how did your date on Sunday go?"

"It wasn't great, definitely not what I expected, and before you ask, I did not have sex, Sari. Not that it's any of your business anyway."

"I'm just looking out for you, Liv. I don't want to see you get hurt. I am a little jealous, though. I was hoping to be the one to help you fix your little problem, babe."

"First of all, it is not a little problem. It is huge. Secondly, what good would that do us? We don't need to bring sex into our friendship. I don't want to lose you."

"I didn't mean to downplay your trauma, Liv. I'm sorry." Genuinely curious, Sari asked Olivia, "Why would you lose me if we had sex? I'm not going anywhere. You are stuck with me forever, babe. Now, come over here and let me hold you."

Rising out of her chair, a little wobbly from all the wine and whiskey that evening, Olivia settled herself on Sari's lap, allowing herself to be wrapped tight in strong arms that made her feel safe. She knew that it was probably wrong of her to do so, the guilt rolling slowly through her delayed senses, but she sunk into the embrace any-way, letting Sari's face rest against her neck.

19

With her bags packed for the island, Olivia paced her living room, nervously waiting for Sari, Dave, and Gail to arrive, trying to envision how this first tour was going to go. Not everyone was needed at this early stage of construction as all the establishments were not fully completed yet. Olivia hadn't seen any of it in person yet. The first and only time that she had been on the island they had been transporting the heavy equipment to begin construction and supplies that were needed to build the structures. She was not an equipment expert or a building engineer, so she left that to the RED to choose whom they thought would be best suited for those jobs. She would step in when it was time to run the island and begin bringing people into the program. Right now, they needed to see how things were progressing. The community complexes had been completed, along with the health center. She believed that they had just finished the structural portion of the resident living quarters and were on to the cosmetic part. She wasn't sure though how far the crews had gotten on the employee living quarters, or the security building and posts. There wasn't much that could be done until those were complete. There were some other minor buildings that needed to be built for storage but that could be done with residents on the island. The timeline to begin accepting residents was getting closer by the day, and it was time to crack the whip if need be.

The last week had been wonderful, fun-filled, and full of surprises watching Molly's kittens Ginger, Smoke, and Shadow grow. Olivia was a bit sad to have to leave for a week, but this was part of her new life. She had conceived this project and now it was happening. The upcoming press release did have her a bit worried but she was sure that it would be fine. Her mind was spinning out of control, and she thought, Focus. It's time to get your head in the game. Almost go-time. She was so thankful to hear her doorbell, knowing that it must be Gail, because either of the other two would just knock and walk in.

"Hello Gail. How are you today?"

"I'm good. Nervous but good. I had my husband drop me off so there wouldn't be so many cars clogging up your driveway."

"How thoughtful of you. Come in and have a seat. The others should be arriving at any time."

"I am so thankful that you chose me to be a part of this project. It is something that I am passionate about as well. Cleaning up our streets for our children is so important."

Hearing Sari's car pull in the driveway, Olivia nodded. "I love that you are so passionate about this project. It was one of the reasons that I chose you." Moving to the door, she said, "Please excuse me. I need to see them in." She opened the door for both Sari and Dave, showing them to the living room where Gail was already seated.

"As you all know, our deadline to begin admitting residents is rapidly approaching, so we need to make sure that the construction is on schedule and up to the standards that I have set. Each of you has your own area to assess. You need to figure out your timeline and make sure that it fits the start date. One month from today, we will be taking in residents onto the island. Their needs must be met, or we will be shut down, and that's not an option, which is why I chose each of you as supervisors. You are the best in your fields. I believe that you will help me make the island a success. Do you have any questions about this trip and what you will need to accomplish?"

Dave raised his hand sheepishly. "Why aren't all of the supervisors going over to see the island on this excursion?"

"Good question, Dave. Sari needs to make sure that all of the security buildings and equipment are up to par. Gail has to inspect the residents' living quarters to ensure they meet the requirements, and you have to make sure that all of the intake and application offices are set and ready to handle the influx of residents smoothly. As of right now, the other programs are not essential to construction. They have office space, but without residents, there won't be much for them to do. Zek and Ameera are currently working from home, planning their programs and how they wish to implement them on the island. They will be coming over a week before intake begins to situate their areas and to finalize anything that may need to be changed to accommodate the needs of their personalized programs. We will all be going over at that time. Once residents are on the island, we will all be staying for a minimum of two weeks, with two days back home and then back for another two weeks. We need to be there as much as possible during the opening month to troubleshoot and make sure that the system flows smoothly."

Dave's eyes grew wide at the thought. "I guess I didn't really think about the time away from home being that long."

"She warned you about that so many times, man! What's wrong with you?" Sari questioned, irritation showing through her fierce eyes.

Glaring back at Sari, Dave said, "I don't want to back out. I'm just saying that it's a long time away. Tammy won't like it at all."

"That's her problem then, isn't it? My bet is that she just won't like that you and Ameera are there on an island together and she will be stuck back here."

"We don't even see Ameera anymore. She walked away about a week ago. She said she was bored with us because Tammy's jealousy was tiring."

Sari nodded. "I can totally see that. It is annoying. I don't know how you put up with it, especially since she's the one that wants to date other people."

"People, can we focus please?" Olivia said. "The shuttle will be here any minute to take us to the helipad. Do you have any relevant questions that I can answer before we leave?"

Looking at Olivia meekly, Sari asked, "Can we see the kittens?"

Shocked into laughter, Olivia shook her head. "They are sleeping quietly. I don't want to disturb them. Molly is so tired from caring for them and Max is tired from worrying about all of them so much. Before I came out here, all five of them were curled up together fast asleep in their bed. If that's all, then grab your bags, ladies and gentlemen. The shuttle just pulled up. We are off to the beautiful island of Euphoria."

The drive to the helipad was uneventful, though a bit long, the scenery passing by quickly in the windows. Pulling up to a large, fenced area, the shuttle stopped at a gate and was greeted by a uniformed military officer. Showing his ID, the driver was allowed to pass through and take them the rest of the way to the helipad.

Sari and the others looked at Olivia, a bit surprised at the level of security, to which Olivia responded, "We are working for RED directly now. This island will be well secured both here on the mainland and at the island level. Sari, this is your area, overseeing security and technology. We do not want people to try to get on or off island without permission. This isn't a resort, like some seem to think. It is an option for those that wish to choose this way of life, but removed from the mainland, where they could cause harm to others that wish to remain free and clear of drugs like Ink."

The weight of responsibility sinking in heavily, Sari replied, "I knew security would be tight. I guess I just didn't fully put the entirety of the island and how people would react to it into perspective. I see what you are saying, and the necessity for high security. I will make sure the system runs smoothly."

Alert now, having been woken when they stopped at the gate, Dave looked around, nodding to himself. "This is almost an alternative to jailing some people, isn't it, Liv?"

"Yes, some of the officials are looking at it that way. Instead of placing a drug offender in the jail system, they will be sent to the island for a predetermined amount of time. Once that time is up, they can go back to the mainland and stay out of trouble, or they may choose to sign the contract and stay on the island, living as they wish."

Curious about the PR aspect, Sari wondered aloud, "How is this different from jail if they cannot come and go as they please?"

"On Euphoria residents are not confined to a cell. They do not get an hour per day outside in the sunshine. On Euphoria our residents are free to walk the island, join activities through the community building center, build relationships, and lead mostly free lives. Residents that are sent over through the court system do have a set time to be on the island, but again, they are not being confined other than not being able to leave the island. That is for the safety of everyone involved."

Curiously, Gail asked, "How many people are we able to house on the island? I realize that it is a large island, but I would imagine that it will fill quickly with what is being offered."

"The island is set up to house mainly people who are addicted to Ink and do not want to get clean, but not exclusively. We will be accepting some applicants from other groups as well. Dave, that is your area. You will need to balance the number of residents of each type of user to fit a predetermined ratio that will be given to you by the RED."

"I can do that once I have the information, but what about marijuana users? Will we be allowing them residency on the island?"

"That is a great question, and the short answer is no. We will not offer space to people for marijuana, psilocybin, or cocaine, as all of these drugs are now legal in our nation, and being regulated by the government, because they are naturally occurring."

"So, what you are saying is that it is the most dangerous drugs that we will be handing out to the island residents," Gail said.

"Yes, that is correct. We will give residents a specific ration each day that will be determined once they enter the intake process. This is not just a place for them to land softly, so they can do any number of drugs that they wish all day long. They will receive rations, but everyone will have a job per se, and we have employees, led by Ameera, that will encourage the residents to get healthy, to teach them how to be healthy. We understand that this will not work for everyone and that some may not flourish in the program. However, that is their personal choice, and we will not be forcing anyone to do anything that they choose not to do. This is not a rehabilitation center. It is a safe place for these people to live the life that they want without harming others or being constantly ridiculed."

As they grabbed their bags and got out of the shuttle, the responsibility weighed heavily on them all, knowing that this was an opportunity to make a difference in so many people's lives, but also realizing how easily and quickly this entire project could go south. Olivia shouldered this weight well, possibly because it was her idea, or maybe because she had deeper personal reasons, but the others looked at her with newfound respect and walked up the stairs to the helipad with her, ready to embrace what the island had to offer.

Excitedly, they entered the helicopter, securing their luggage and strapping themselves in tight, placing the headphones over their ears, awaiting takeoff. As the helicopter lifted into the sky, Olivia looked out her window, seeing the ground fall slowly away as they rose higher and higher before heading out to sea. The grassy land soon gave way to sand and beach, and then there was nothing except the vast blue ocean. Pointing and laughing excitedly, Olivia saw a pod of whales breaching the surface, swimming slow and steady. They stayed up long enough for each of them to see the beautiful creatures emerge from the depths, water splashing and shining on their massive bodies, before diving back down to the safety of the oceanic depths. Searching the ocean surface for more creatures, the crew passed the time in silent awe of the endless blue that they were seeing—not a speck of land in sight.

Dave asked, "Is by helicopter the only way to get to the island, Liv?"

"No, you can get there by boat as well, but helicopters are much faster and therefore more efficient for smaller groups. When residents start arriving, as well as our regular staff, they will likely be brought by boat. The supervisors will all be on island by that time, brought over by this means of transportation."

Gail called out, "Look! Over there. I see land. Is that the island, Olivia?"

"Yes, ma'am, it is." Olivia smiled broadly with pride. "Welcome to Euphoria, the island that will help shape a new future for our nation and allow people freedoms that they have never been given before. A safe space that many will be able to call home. Our future and the future of our careers wait for us down there. No pressure, right? Haha."

The pilot made a slow circle of the entire island, allowing the crew to see the sheer size of it. The island was mostly circular with a mix of palm trees and hardwood. They had done their best to maintain nature's landscaping. The crew could see the dirt roads that wound their way through the natural landscape of the island from building to building. The island was twenty miles in diameter, and they could see where the warehouse area was in a crescent-shaped harbor on one end of the island. On the opposite side there was the intake area where the boats could come and dock from the mainland. Most of the edges of the island were cliffs and bluffs but there were a couple areas where the sun shone invitingly on the sandy beaches.

The dark-colored roofs of the housing communities peeked through the treetops, and the crew could see where their residents were going to be living. At this time there were five complete communities that would be filled first. The communities were spread out in different areas of the island so as not to have too much congestion in one place. The central intake building was fairly close to the community center that would house the health services and coordinate activities for residents. The staff housing was near one of the beaches that was further removed from the rest of the structures to enable staff to have the feeling of separation from work.

Olivia glowed as she looked over the island and back at her staff. Pride swelled in her chest as she saw the looks of amazement and awe on their faces. Smiling broadly, she quipped, "Not a bad place to work, huh?"

After the pilot carefully landed and shut down the engine, Olivia and her crew grabbed their luggage and hopped out of the helicopter, looking around in awe at the scene that lay out in front of them. It was so modern and businesslike, yet peaceful. So much like a resort.

They made their way into the building through the doorway that led to a stairwell and elevator. Wanting to drop off their bags and allow them to settle a bit, Olivia took them to the fifth and top floor first. She motioned for them to follow and showed them a hallway that was reminiscent of a hotel as she explained, "Supervisors will have their own suites here on the fifth floor, and regular workers are down one level and have personal rooms but share common spaces." She showed each of them to their personal suites before entering her own, taking it all in for the first time.

Her suite was facing the ocean, a large window offering an amazing view outside. She took in the small but modern kitchenette, large flat-screen television on the wall of the attached living room area, and plush blue sofa sitting against the other wall next to the door to the bedroom, where a queen-size bed sat in the center of the room. There was a roomy closet on one side near the bathroom entrance, and the other wall was a large sliding glass door that led to a small balcony that held a wrought iron table and chair set overlooking the ocean with a view of the gardens below as well. Making her way to the bathroom, she found a jacuzzi tub along with a stand-up shower, all frosted and colored glass, throwing rainbows everywhere. Boy, they did not cut any corners here, Olivia thought, a bit shocked at her personal accommodations here on the island. Heading back out into the hallway to meet the others near the elevator, she wondered if their rooms were as lavish as hers.

Seeing the rest of the group already waiting for her, she smiled and asked, "Are your rooms to your liking?"

Instant agreement came from everyone, all exclaiming how lovely the rooms were, how it was like being on vacation, even though it was really for work. They raved about the comfort of the beds and sofas. The happiness flowing through the group made her feel good. Having such beautiful rooms to escape to when needed would make for a less stressful work environment. Pressing the elevator button, Olivia moved them to the ground level to begin the island facility tour. She led them outside to an orange jeep that was sitting out front, motioning for everyone to get in. She hopped in the driver's seat, started the engine, and headed to the interior of the island on well-managed dirt roads.

The drive was short, and they arrived at what looked like a small village of tiny houses. Turning to look at everyone, she explained, "This is one of the resident housing areas. Each house is set up for either a single person or a couple and has only one bedroom equipped with a couch that folds out into a full-size bed and a bathroom. As of right now, there are ten housing areas scattered around the island. Gail, this is the area that you and your staff will monitor, assigning houses and helping residents get settled. Also, if there are any housing disputes, they will fall under your department as well. Let's move on."

Driving even farther inland, Olivia brought them to a large building with multiple entrances, with signs above each entrance to clarify directions, letting you know which way to go. "This is the community growth area. Ezekiel, Zek for short, will run a portion of this area. Also, within this building is security, your area, Sari. There is also a gym, the wellness center, and the distribution center, which is Ameera's area. One of the important things to know is that the distribution center dispenses the daily allotment of both narcotics and food. All other housing needs will be handled by Gail and the Resident Housing Department, working alongside the Resident Intake Department."

Looking around in awe of the establishment, taking in all the amenities, thinking about the sheer amount of money that it took to build as well as run this island, the group sat in stunned silence until Dave finally asked, "Who in the world is paying for all of this?"

Olivia looked at all of them. "The people that want the drugs off the streets, to make our region safe again, and our government. That's what I am told anyway," she said, her eyes drifting over the landscape while she thought of the enormity of this project. *It had better not fail,* she thought, *or I will be ruined, and so will everyone that has chosen to work with me.*

20

The days had flown by, surveying and adjusting, making sure that systems were getting set up properly. There had not been much downtime on Euphoria for the crew over the last week. They fell into bed each night exhausted, only to get up the next morning and begin the cycle again. The first stint on Euphoria was finally complete for the team and Olivia was thrilled to be almost home. The shuttle from the helipad was only minutes away from delivering her to her doorstep now. She couldn't wait to see her cats and to see how much the kittens had grown, even though Hannah had sent her pictures every day. She was looking forward to having a week at home before having to go back to the island, and looking over at her coworkers, she could see the relief of soon being home on their faces as well. Not that it was awful on Euphoria, but there was a lot of work to be done before they could accept residents, and it wasn't like they could enjoy the downtime on the island, because right now there was none.

A huge smile spread across her face as the shuttle pulled up to her driveway, letting her and the others out. They had already discussed going straight home from there instead of coming inside. Gail's husband was there waiting with a smile and a beautiful bouquet of flowers for her, making Olivia's heart ache just a bit as she wished that she had that as well. Seeing the emotion play across her face, Sari put an arm around her and squeezed tight, offering comfort and love before heading off to drop Dave at home.

Walking quickly to her front door, Olivia rushed inside, dropping her bags once inside, and made her way to the bedroom closet. Peering in, she saw her sweet kitty family minus Max. She crouched down and stroked Molly's head, cooing at her lovingly, fingers gently petting the kittens that seemed to have doubled in size. Hearing a noise across the hall, Olivia walked to the guest room and saw Hannah still asleep with Max curled up by her legs. He looked up and mewed quietly, as though not to wake his companion. He got up gently and weaved himself between Olivia's legs, wanting to be picked up. She obliged and carried him to the living room to grab her bags and then back to the bedroom so she could get settled and maybe take a nap. It was nice having laundry facilities on the island, because it meant she didn't have to do a ton of laundry every time she came home from work. She put away her clothes and stored her bags until the following week. Olivia yawned and stretched, deciding that a nap was indeed called for. She removed her clothes and climbed between her soft, silky sheets, snuggling way down with Max curling up next to her side, purring softly.

The scent of bacon and coffee drifted into Olivia's sleep, coaxing her awake with their tantalizing aroma, speaking directly to her stomach, which was now growling loudly. Rolling over to look at the clock, she realized that she had only slept for an hour, a good nap, but now it was time to get the day started. Hopping out of bed, she grabbed her robe and headed toward the smells that woke her from her slumber. She found Hannah humming in the kitchen, cooking away, unaware that she was no longer alone in the room. Turning to grab the plate off the kitchen island, she screamed when she saw Olivia, spatula clattering to the floor, sending eggs everywhere. Olivia began laughing hysterically, apologizing at the same time while moving to help Hannah clean up the mess that was made. Hand to her heart still, Hannah grabbed a cloth from the sink and wiped up what was left of the mess, hurrying to remove the pan from the heat so the eggs wouldn't burn. Olivia reached for the coffee mugs, filled them, and brought them out to the porch, saying, "It's a perfect morning to eat outside."

Hannah nodded. "That was my original plan as well. I was going to wake you when it was finished and surprise you with breakfast."

"That is very sweet of you. You really go above and beyond for me."

"I love being here, taking care of the house and the cats. It's so much nicer than the apartment I share in the city. I mean, the apartment is a decent size with three bedrooms, but then my roommates bring people over and it gets loud, and I really don't care to hear them in the middle of the night. The walls are so paper thin."

"I can see where that would be annoying. One of my favorite things about my home is that it's secluded and quiet. I like my privacy. I'm sure you will find your perfect place one day."

"I hope it's just like this, Olivia, really. You have made this into the most relaxing, zen-like place to live. I am always at peace here. It makes it hard to go back to my apartment after I've been here, probably more so now since it's been a week this time."

"You will be spending a lot of time here over the next few months. Hopefully, the times at your apartment aren't too awful for you."

"I know this is a silly, crazy idea, but would you ever consider having a roommate here?"

Taken a bit by surprise, Olivia responded slowly. "I haven't ever really considered it. I like my privacy." Laughing a little, she added, "I prefer to walk around naked. I find clothing extremely restrictive, so I'm not sure how any potential roommate would feel about that."

"Oh, I wouldn't care one bit! You're gorgeous. Not that I would be looking. I'm not a lesbian or anything. I wouldn't make it uncomfortable, I swear. I just, I love it here, ugh... I sound like an idiot. Sorry," Hannah stammered, her face turning furiously red.

Resting a hand on her knee, Olivia said, "Hannah, relax, it's alright. First, I don't care if you're a lesbian or not. I would imagine that as an adult, you would be able to restrain yourself. I am thrilled that you love it here because that means that I did a good job creating my space. As for being a roommate, I will seriously consider it since I am going to be gone often, and it would make sense to have someone that I can trust here to make sure that everything is taken care of properly."

Finishing their meal, they relaxed together, both lost in thought, minds wandering over different scenarios. Olivia downed the last swallow of her coffee, scratched Molly on the head, pleased to see that she had taken some time away from the babies to eat, and contemplated what she wanted to do for the day. A swim at some point would happen for sure, and maybe some gardening, but right now, yoga. She needed to get active and work her muscles. Grabbing a bottle from the cupboard, Olivia filled it with water, looking out at Hannah sitting on the porch, eyes closed, soaking up the sun, thinking that she really was a good girl, and good company. Maybe having someone here would be alright. She walked to her room, finding shorts that fit like a second skin, short and tight, a sports bra that would hold her well, but not constrict her horribly, and her yoga mat. She gathered her items up and headed out to the patio by the pool. Setting the outside speakers to play meditation music, she opened her mat and began. Yoga was one of her favorite ways to work out, creating both strength and flexibility, clearing the mind and giving her a peaceful feeling within.

Hannah called out from the porch, "Do you mind if I join you?"

"Feel free. There are spare yoga mats in the pool house."

Finding a mat, Hannah brought it over near Olivia and spread out, beginning her own yoga exercises, quiet and contemplative. Olivia noticed that she almost seemed to want guidance or needed an older woman's attention. This made Olivia wonder about her relationship with her mother, but she did not ask or comment on it. For an hour, they stretched and bent, testing their bodies' strength, pushing them to do more, hold more poses, and be stronger. They were both sweaty but relaxed when they finished.

"I'm going to jump in the pool to cool off. You're welcome to join," Olivia said as Hannah was picking up her mat.

"That sounds great! Let me just put this away first. I don't have my suit with me, though. Is there one that I can borrow?"

"I am sure there is one somewhere in the pool house if you want to search. Just so you know, I'm swimming naked," Olivia stated, pulling her shorts and bra off while standing in front of Hannah, thinking, What better time than now to see if she can handle how I live?

Looking away and then back at Olivia, then toward the pool house, not sure where to rest her eyes, Hannah stared hard at the ground, cheeks flushed as Olivia dove into the pool with a tiny splash. Olivia watched her go into the pool house while she began to swim laps, wondering if her swimming naked may have changed Hannah's mind about staying there. In Olivia's eyes there was no reason to be uncomfortable with nakedness. Everyone was beautiful in their own way. It was just a body, one that she took pride in and cared for. But that wasn't for everybody. Look at Claudia for instance. She was a heavy woman, but stunning in her own right. So stunning that drop-dead gorgeous Sari had had sex with her often over that week in the field. Olivia wondered if they had ever gotten together again after that, but it wasn't her business, so she hadn't asked.

Hearing a noise come from the edge of the pool, Olivia looked up and saw Hannah standing at the stairway, wearing an aqua blue bikini that complemented her tanned skin, her long wavy blonde hair pulled back into a braid.

Shrugging shyly, Hannah said, "It was the one that fit best, but I don't have much of a chest to fill it out like you do."

"Oh honey, you look like a model, seriously. Who says you need to have large breasts, anyway? I like your shape. It's perky and fit. You should be proud of it."

"You're just saying that to make me feel good. I'm alright, but I'm not that great-looking. I have like no curves to my body."

"You listen to me, Hannah. I used to date a woman that had the same build as you. She was the most beautiful creature that I ever laid eyes on." The past snuck up on Olivia quiet and quick like a big cat going in for the kill. Her hands running over smooth tanned skin, over her shoulders, up and down the arms, then moving to cup breasts that fit her hands perfectly. Thumbs slowly circling nipples, pulling a low moan from her love. The sound of passion lighting a fire in her belly. She dipped her head down to draw that nipple into her mouth as her hand slipped down between the valley of her lover's legs, finding it wet and inviting.

Sucking in a breath, Olivia came rushing back to the present, aware that Hannah was looking at her, slightly concerned. "You do have curves, soft quiet ones, the kind that sneak up on a person and throw them for the biggest loop because they weren't expecting to feel so exhilarated by them."

"Wait, what? You are a lesbian? I didn't know that. Not that I care. I'm totally cool with that. I find it intriguing. You really think I'm pretty?"

Shocked into laughter by Hannah's innocent rambling, Olivia replied, "I'm not a lesbian, I'm bisexual, and I think you're far more than just pretty, Hannah. You're beautiful."

"You're so nice to me, Olivia." Hannah paused and then asked, "So, if you like men and women, how do you decide who to date?"

Olivia considered the question, not wanting to rush an answer. She thought about her past relationships, especially her most recent one. She had planned on being married by now to the love of her life, a woman that she'd believed was strong and beautiful, much like Hannah. She thought of the disappointment that Joe had created within her. Men were always more difficult for her anyway. Sadness grew in her heart as the impact of her past love life settled deep in her chest. She replied softly, "I don't decide because I don't date anyone anymore."

"What about that Joe guy that dropped stuff off for the cats while you were gone? He is really good-looking."

"He is good-looking, but we are not dating." Changing the subject, Olivia asked, "What did he bring for the cats?"

"He brought some toys and cat food that he said Molly really enjoyed when she was at the shelter. He is such a nice guy!" Hannah gushed.

"I would agree. He is supposed to be stopping by later to check in on the kittens."

"I can make sure that I am out of your way. You know, so you can have privacy."

"There is no need for that, especially if you are going to be staying with me for a while."

"Are you serious? You are going to let me move in here with you? Yes! Thank you so much!"

"We still need to discuss details and such. I wasn't sure how you would react to my habits, but you handled my undressing and swimming well, so I figured that we could give it a shot. A trial run for now. No need to tell your current roommates at this point. Let's just see how the next week goes, and then I have to go back to the island for a couple of weeks this time."

"Okay, no problem! I am so excited. You really have no idea how much I love it here. I have the ability to work from home thankfully. It isn't too complicated with medical records and insurance. As long as I have a good internet connection and a stable phone line I'm set."

"Great! We should probably get out before we turn into prunes," Olivia suggested, swimming for the stairs. Reaching for her towel by the lounge chair, she placed it over the cushions, lying down to soak in the sun and relax for a bit. Opening one eye, she saw Hannah staring at her from the edge of the pool, walking over to a lounge chair to lie down as well, unable to resist looking over Olivia's naked body.

Catching her eye, Hannah apologized. "I'm sorry, I don't mean to keep staring, it just baffles me how you can be so comfortable in your own skin like that. I mean, like I said, you are gorgeous, but you aren't at all self-conscious about being totally naked in front of me."

"There is no reason to be self-conscious in front of anybody. It doesn't matter who you are. Everyone should be comfortable in their own skin."

"Well, I'm not. Even when I'm alone, I feel funny being naked if I'm not showering or something."

"That's no way to be. You are a beautiful woman. Do you want to learn how?"

"Learn how to what?"

"Learn how to be comfortable naked, silly."

"I mean, I guess I could try. I don't know if it will work, though."

"Take off your suit, and let the sun touch your body, all of it."

"I'm not sure I can do that."

"Then don't, but if you want to learn, you just have to jump in and try. It makes no difference to me either way. It is nice though, being comfortable." She closed her eyes and leaned her head back, knowing that Hannah's eyes were roaming her body. "If you want, I can help."

"I could probably use a little help," Hannah said meekly.

Olivia stood face-to-face with Hannah. "Close your eyes and trust me."

Olivia watched as Hannah took a deep breath and closed her eyes. She could see her tremble slightly with nervousness. Olivia spoke gently. "I am going to remove your suit. Keep your eyes closed. I will guide you to the lounge chair where you will lay back and relax. Is that alright?"

Unable to speak, Hannah nodded slowly, biting her lips with anxiety.

Olivia slowly moved her hands to the bikini top, reaching around to untie the strings that held it in place. As they came loose, she let the material fall into her hands before setting it aside. Then she slid her fingers under the waistband of the bottoms, slowly slipping them down Hannah's long golden-brown legs where they lay in a pool of material at her feet. Upon standing back up Olivia saw Hannah's breasts quiver slightly as she took a breath which stirred a small feeling of desire inside of Olivia. Her face grew hot, and she immediately felt guilty as she was supposed to simply be helping Hannah feel comfortable. The resemblance between Hannah's body and Aria's was somewhat uncanny, causing some surprising reactions within Olivia. She guided her over to the lounge and helped her sit and lay back. Once Hannah was settled and comfortable Olivia went back to her own lounge chair to lie in the sun.

"Maybe I should just put my bikini back on," Hannah whispered.

Olivia, her voice as soft as a caress, said gently, "Hannah, trust me. Close your eyes." She waited for her to follow directions, then said, "Good, now let your hands fall to your sides." Olivia patiently waited for Hannah to allow her hands to fall away from her body, which she did after a few moments. "Now take a couple deep breaths and let yourself relax. Feel the warm sun on your body, especially in those places that it normally doesn't get to touch." Olivia watched Hannah's face closely to see her reaction, seeing the worry lines slowly begin to fade, noticing her body becoming loose and more relaxed, and finally seeing a small smile on her face. "That's it, right there. Feel how nice that is, the warmth, the sun, the freedom to embrace your own body. Hold on to that feeling. Sleeping naked also helps with feeling confident in your body. You should try that too."

"Oh, I am definitely going to. Thank you so much for showing me how to do this. It feels amazing and liberating. I don't know if I could be this comfortable in front of anybody else, but even if I can just by myself or with you, it's great!"

"I am happy that I could help. Don't ever let anyone make you feel ashamed of your body. It's beautiful, just like you."

Olivia glanced over, taking in Hannah's long wavy blonde hair and cute and perky body, wondering who had put the idea into this woman's head that she wasn't good enough just because she didn't have big tits or porn-star curves. Disgust at society and their standards and norms rushed in, something that she really tried to avoid thinking about too much because it fueled anger inside. Riding on that tide of anger was also guilt. The guilt that she, at one time, had expected Aria to fit the mold that she wanted her to, to fit the life that she wanted. So much so that it had destroyed them both.

21

The kittens were trying to crawl all over the place now, so for their safety, Olivia had a space built near the catio door for them to stay until they got bigger. The wall was high enough that they couldn't get out, but Molly and Max could go in and out of their enclosure as they pleased. This exasperated Ginger, Smoke, and Shadow because they wanted to see the whole world. Olivia's love for them grew daily, each of them having their own personality quirks, and so playful that they warmed her heart. Thinking back on daily life for the last two weeks, it had been interesting.

Sharing her home with someone was not something that she was used to, but it seemed to be working out alright. Hannah was a good girl, her confidence growing daily. Olivia felt great affection for her now, watching her blossom and grow under her guidance. There were some odd occurrences that partially raised red flags, but hopefully they didn't mean anything, and if they did, then oh well. Olivia had no desire to get twisted up in some mess right when she was about to launch Euphoria. Her career was the most important thing in her life at this point.

Turning her attention to work, she ran through a mental list of items to get together for her next trip to the island. She had a massive list of names, compiled by the RED for Dave to run through, so he could pick out the first group of residents that were going to be welcomed to the island. The housing assignments would be worked out by Gail and her department, and security was almost up to the standards set by the RED and had been gone over intensely by Sari. The others all had their own areas to contend with as well over the next week.

One week left. Only one week until they would be ushering residents onto the island.

She shook her head, thinking that sometimes it all seemed so crazy to her that this was even happening, that her proposal for the island had even been accepted, and that she was running the entire project. There had been some protesting over the last week when they went public with Euphoria, explaining how it worked, the purpose of the island, and instructions on how to apply to live there. The sound of her phone going off pulled her out of her thoughts. She ignored it at first, wanting to prepare for the trip, but it continued incessantly.

Seeing that it was from the RED, she answered quickly. "Good morning, Olivia here. How can I help you?"

"Olivia, we need you to get to the helipad as soon as possible. There is a group of protesters at the gates. We are holding a press conference in two hours. Be there." The call ended without a goodbye.

Hearing her doorbell ring drew Olivia out of her work trance and back to reality. Making her way down the hall, she wondered who it could be. Listening, she heard Hannah getting up to answer the door, words being spoken quietly so she wasn't able make them out. Turning the corner into the living room, she saw Joe standing by the front door speaking with Hannah, reaching up to brush a stray strand of hair out of her face, making Hannah smile but step back. Clearing her throat so that they would be aware that she was standing there, Olivia looked questioningly at Joe, trying to decide whether he was flirting with her young roommate or just being kind. He smiled broadly at her, not acting guilty at all, but Hannah shrunk back, looking extremely uncomfortable, turning, and heading to her room, shutting the door firmly.

"I may have embarrassed her," Joe laughed.

Olivia asked, "What are you doing here? I wasn't expecting you today."

"I knew you would be leaving for a couple of weeks, so I wanted to stop and see you. Why doesn't it feel like you want to see me?"

"It's not that, I'm just terribly busy getting everything together before I leave this evening. I have a lot to go over in the next couple of hours."

"Olivia, I know that this is a big deal for you, but you really make me feel like I am not a priority in your life. You have more passion for the cats than you do for me, it seems. I've been trying to give you time and space to figure it out, but I feel like you won't ever want me the way I want you."

Hand on hip, face impassive, Olivia responded, "So you chose now to do this? Now? When I am about to leave for two weeks? When I just specifically told you that I do not have any spare time today? You throw this at me right now?"

Shrugging like a guilty child, Joe commented quietly, "Maybe you can figure it out while you are gone. I don't want to wait forever for you to be ready to have a relationship with me. If you are ever ready. I've been patient, Olivia. I like you, but I can't keep putting my life on hold."

"I see. I thought that we were friends, and never once did I imply that you wait around for me. Have a good day, Joe. I have things to finish before I leave," she said, opening the door and holding it for him to exit, her body language clearly saying, do not touch me.

Head down, Joe walked down the driveway to his car, looking back once before driving away. Olivia, shaking with irritation, closed the door gently, wanting to slam it with all her might, but refraining. She returned her focus to work, to what truly mattered in her life. Walking back to her room, she encountered Hannah stepping out of her bedroom, looking upset.

"Olivia, I swear I wasn't flirting or anything. I hope you aren't mad at me or anything. I didn't know that he was going to do that with my hair."

"Hannah, stop. It's fine," Olivia said.

"Oh no, it's not like that, Olivia. Please don't make me leave here. I swear we've only flirted a few times and it didn't mean anything."

Sighing heavily, Olivia said, "Hannah, I am not concerned about it, really. I cannot give him what he needs, and he can't fix me. He and I are just friends, nothing more."

"What do you mean he can't fix you? What's wrong? Are you alright?" Concern clear in Hannah's voice and all over her face.

"I am fine, nothing to worry about. Do you have everything that you'll need while I am gone? I have everything set up for the cats."

Clearly not convinced, but not wanting to upset her benefactor, Hannah shook her head yes. "Do you want to go for a swim or something before you leave? It might be nice to just hang out and relax."

"Thank you, but no. I only have about an hour before the shuttle will be here to pick me up. You go ahead though, if you want to. It'll be a beautiful day for a swim," Olivia said, walking into her room, gathering all her folders and placing them in her rolling file case next to her luggage. Rummaging around some more, she could hear Hannah move through the house, likely on her way to the pool.

Letting her mind wander back over the last two weeks to the many times that Joe was over, Olivia remembered seeing him searching Hannah out, remembered lust filling his eyes as they roamed her body, remembered his funny and flirtatious comments toward her. It was obvious that he wanted her in at least a physical way. Olivia knew that Hannah was beautiful, so she couldn't condemn him for that. But then today he'd touched her.

If Olivia thought hard about it, it made sense. Joe and Hannah were closer in age, both of them probably wanted a family, and both were particularly good-looking and good people. Olivia had never really been fair to him, using him for her own secret needs, trying to heal herself with his friendship and kindness. Moving her bags out into the living room by the front door to await the shuttle, she went to the kitchen and stood at the back door, looking out at Hannah in the pool, naked. Smiling and feeling pride in helping the confidence in Hannah bloom and grow, Olivia thought, If he hurts her, I will kill him, already knowing that they would end up together in one way or another. Olivia called out to Hannah, "I have to go now. See you in a couple weeks," blowing her a kiss as she turned and made her way out of the house.

Climbing into the back seat of the shuttle after stowing her luggage in the back, Olivia saw that Sari was already on board. The nervousness that Olivia was experiencing only multiplied when she saw her friend. What if I fail? What if I am not capable of convincing the public that Euphoria is a great opportunity for everyone, not just addicts? Where will that leave the lives of everyone involved in this project? She felt a lump forming in her throat, and she attempted to push it down, but Sari could already see it and pulled Olivia over, holding her tight as the van started to drive away from her house. Stroking her arms and back, kissing her hair, whispering that it would all be just fine. Sari let Olivia take the strength that she needed as tears flowed down her face, knowing that she would talk when she was ready, but not until then. With her eyes dried by the time they reached the compound, Olivia still held on to Sari's hand, needing familiarity and stability. Making a vow to herself to never mess up this friendship in any way.

Getting to the entrance of the helipad location was difficult to say the least as there were crowds of protestors surrounding the van. Security was having issues keeping the crowd under control as they pulled up to the gate. They could hear the chanting and yelling from outside of the van. These people were passionate about not allowing the project to move forward. Some of them showed sadness but most of the protesters seemed angry. That passion distorted their faces into hate-filled masks. They threw objects at the van and tried to open the doors, slamming their fists on the exterior. Many of them held signs that ranged from Stop wasting our tax dollars to Be a drug addict, get a free vacation with a no symbol. Live for free and do me with an image of Ink was plastered on many of the signs.

Olivia and her team were fearful for a moment but soon security was finally able to get the crowd back far enough for the van to get through the gates without letting the protestors in. As they pulled around Olivia could see that the stage was set for the press conference, but it did not look like it was going to be received well. Olivia sighed deeply. She had known that this would come. She just wasn't quite ready with everything else that was going on in her life. She squared her shoulders and made her way out of the van and to the stage to meet with the members of RED before taking her place front and center.

Thankfully the press conference was only open to the media outlets, but they were eating up the material that the protestors were giving them for their breaking news stories. She could see the cameras panning between the stage and the gates where the swarms of people were shouting and waving their signs. Being given the go-ahead to begin, Olivia approached the podium, standing tall with strength and pride. Stepping to center stage, she began. "Welcome, everyone. I would like to take a moment to thank you all for taking time out of your busy days to come out for this press release. As you already know, Euphoria is set to begin admitting residents in the very near future. We have the facilities prepared to meet the needs of our residents and we are in the process of selecting them currently. I know that you have an abundance of questions so I will do my best to answer them as clearly as possible in the amount of time that we have together this evening. Who is first?"

Questions were fired immediately, the reporters all speaking at once, vying for the first position.

"How is building a place for addicts to live and do drugs beneficial to society?"

"Why are you forcing birth control on residents?"

"How do you justify spending billions of taxpayer dollars to provide free living arrangements and Ink to residents?"

"What kind of medical care can be expected for residents?"

"Who is funding this project?"

Olivia took the questions in and pondered how to answer them all. "How many of you believe in freedom? Everyone should since it is what our nation's foundation is built on. This doesn't mean that only some people are free to choose how to live, but all people. These addicts as you call them are people too, people who have chosen a different life path than you. Who are we to tell them how to live their lives? We can only support them in the best way possible. Many of the people of our nation have been asking and then demanding that we address and fix the drug epidemic that we are facing. This has the potential to not only answer the call made by the people of our nation, but to allow for the easement of the justice system which is currently overpopulated. This will help with the funding of Euphoria along with grants and other capital funds that we have received. As for the health and well-being of our residents, they will receive routine medical care along with community-building opportunities that resemble life on the mainland. Now, even though we have a medical center on the island, we are not equipped to handle pregnancies. This is why each resident must be fitted with an implant. This is not nor will it ever be optional as we cannot have children on the island for their own safety." More questions were raised by the reporters, but Olivia felt she had said enough for the time being, "Thank you for your time. No more questions. Have a good evening." She walked off the stage the same way she had walked onto it, head held high with confidence that did not show the deep well of anxiety and fear within. She could hear the reporters protesting and calling out to her, some respectfully and others thowing rude comments her way. She hadn't looked at the statistics recently, but from the sounds of this crowd the approval ratings were dropping. Suddenly there was a roar from the crowd. The protesters had broken through the line and were surging toward the stage. The angry mob was like a tidal wave gaining momentum as they moved. Fear enveloped Olivia as she watched the crowd move toward her, colliding with the line of security that was the only thing between them and the stage. The reporters that had been settled in front of the platform scattered after making sure to capture images of the protestors out of control and rampaging.

It's so much worse than I realized. How many people have I placed in danger?

The emotions began to surge within her again as she felt the weight of the responsibility of the entirety of Euphoria on her shoulders. Sari took her hand as they rushed from the stage to the helicopter without a word, all the other team members already on the island waiting for them to arrive. Not wanting to talk through the headphones, knowing that everyone wearing them would hear, Olivia continued her silence, feeling no need to make small talk, battling the demons within quietly, with Sari watching and waiting with concerned eyes. Olivia leaned her head on Sari's shoulder and sighed, their intertwined fingers resting on her thigh, the ocean below them churning and dark like her mood. How fitting that the weather would be so stormy now, when she herself had such a storm raging inside. It was quite cathartic for her. She knew that it was time to get it all out, so she could move on in peace one way or another. As the helicopter approached the helipad, a strong wind caught it and tossed it around, shaking up the passengers a bit, causing it to circle around again to attempt landing. Looking wide-eyed at Olivia, Sari said, "Babe, I think I'm taking the boat from now on," making her laugh so hard, she doubled over, trying to catch her breath.

"Come on, let's get you to safety," Olivia said, laughing as they stepped down out of the helicopter into the strong ocean wind, clothes whipping back and forth, hair flying everywhere, taking their breath away even while they laughed together. They made their way down into the condominium area, and lugging their suitcases, Sari finally gave in, not able to wait any longer, asking, "What happened, Liv? Are you alright? Do I need to kick someone's ass?"

"I'm good, just feeling bad for and about myself right now. Go get settled and then come over to my place. We can talk then."

Unlocking the door and stepping into her suite, Olivia sighed, looking around, wondering how a job could possibly come with a place like this. She unpacked first so that her clothing wouldn't get wrinkled, then changed into comfy shorts and a tank top, throwing the curtains open wide so she could watch the storm roll in over the island. She waited for Sari to get there, waiting for the right time to speak, waiting for the fire to burn within once again, waiting for the right person to help that fire reignite, always seeming to wait, a frustration burning inside, always waiting and never doing.

Watching the wind lash at the trees, the rain finally pouring down, creating streams along the side of the building, lightning flashing, the sky lighting up as bright as the sun, she stepped out onto the balcony. Feeling the cold rain wash over her skin, the harsh wind tearing at her clothes, her arms outstretched, she welcomed the tempest, willing it to wake the pieces of her body and soul that had gone dormant.

That was how Sari found her. Entering the suite after knocking on the door brought no response. Olivia standing on the balcony, door open, wind and rain whipping in, arms raised to the sky, looking as though she were a goddess calling down the maelstrom. Feeling desire brewing within, Sari pushed it down impatiently and moved to stand beside Olivia in the storm, silent and waiting, knowing that her presence was noticed. Reaching out to grasp her hand, Olivia looked deep into Sari's almond-shaped brown eyes, "Don't ever leave me, okay? I love you and I don't want to know what life without you would be like."

"Liv, babe, I've told you a thousand times, I am not going anywhere. You are stuck with me forever."

"Even if I fail with this project? The public isn't as supportive as they were. It looks like an uphill battle from here."

"You aren't going to fail, Olivia. Euphoria is going to become wildly successful, and we are all going to benefit from it."

"I really hope so, but the pressure is starting to get heavy. What if someone gets hurt during one of the protests, or if the island ends up being a disaster and it makes everything worse?"

Clearly not knowing what to say, Sari swung an arm around Olivia and pulled her close to comfort and give strength. Heads resting together, they stayed like that for a while, letting the storm beat at them, not really feeling the cold penetrate their bodies, watching the lightning play in the sky, bolt after bolt shooting across the entire sky. As the rain began to slow, Olivia looked down at both of them and saw how wet they were. She led Sari inside, grabbing towels for each of them to dry off.

Sitting at the kitchenette bar, she poured a generous three fingers of whisky in a couple of glasses, handing one off to Sari. "On top of that, Joe pulled this ultimatum bullshit with me today after I told him that I didn't have time. Plus, he had been touching Hannah rather affectionately." Olivia took a deep swallow from her own glass. "It's not like Joe hurt me. I don't care about him in that way. I never have. It's myself that I am angry at. I thought I was making progress. I thought I was healing so I could have a full life again, sex and all, thinking that he could give me that back. I was using him for what I wanted, to fix me, without having to do the work."

"Don't be so hard on yourself, Liv. Most people would try the same thing. Some people succeed in thinking that they accomplished healing their traumas only to have them rear their ugly head back up after being in a relationship for a long time, destroying both people in the process. At least you realized it now, instead of later. Maybe he can find happiness with someone else. I think Hannah is way too close to home, but that's just my opinion."

"I don't care what he does, as long as he doesn't hurt her. She is such a sweet girl and just finally building her confidence."

"Did you ever think that maybe that's why he noticed her, because you did such a good job helping her blossom? I mean she is a beautiful girl, but now that she has confidence, she is stunning."

"I suppose it's possible, but I'm thrilled that she is comfortable in her own skin now. I wish I could make that happen for every woman in the world. I wish I could make them all fall in love with their own bodies, be at ease in their own skin, happy when they look in the mirror. Every woman deserves to feel like that."

Holding Olivia's face in her hands, Sari kissed her gently. "That's one of the reasons that I love you so much, Liv. You want to fix the world. And the thing is," Sari whispered, tucking a stray piece of hair behind Olivia's ear, "I believe you can."

Olivia smiled at Sari with appreciation while her thoughts drifted in a different direction.

Does this have more to do with Aria than I realize?

22

Euphoria was absolutely buzzing with energy that morning, with staff hurrying to finish the final touches in their areas, knowing that residents would begin arriving around 10 a.m. They were coming in three separate waves to give the intake team time to process everyone. Each wave of residents comprised twenty-five men and women—chosen by Dave and Claudia, the intake team—that were ideal for the island. There would be residents sent by the judicial system as well, but not for another week, allowing the voluntary residents time to settle in and adjust to their new life. The weather was cooperating, thankfully. The sun was shining, a cool breeze blowing in from the ocean, not a cloud in the sky, the early fog having lifted a short time ago.

All the buildings were ready to receive people, everything set up and organized to run as smooth as silk, though Sari was still running tests on the security and alert systems. Olivia watched as she moved from monitor to monitor, checking and double-checking to make sure that all was as it should be. Walking into the climate-controlled room, Olivia smiled as she approached the rows of technology, in awe that one person knew how to manage all of it. Sari had a small crew for twenty-four-hour surveillance, but it was her baby, and everyone knew it. Seeing Olivia standing by the desk, Sari smiled wide, and with arms spread open said, "Welcome to my lair."

"It looks great, Sari. Not that I really know what everything in this room is. I assume that all the systems are online and ready to go?"

"Yes ma'am, they are. I've run and rerun the tests of all the systems to make sure. When the tech company installed this system, they did a damn good job. No one is getting on or off this island without permission, and if by some miracle they do, we will have pictures and locations immediately, along with the drones that can be released to track them."

"Beautiful. I'm heading over to the community center to check in with Zek and Gail to see how they're doing." Olivia leaned in for a hug and kiss on the cheek. "I will see you later for dinner, right? We are all meeting at my condo."

With a sigh, Sari replied, "I wouldn't miss it for the world, Liv."

Making her way down the hall of the security building, Olivia looked out the windows and took in the landscape before her. The roads were mainly dirt, but smooth. The palm trees reached high up into the sky, and sand was everywhere, giving the island a tropical vacation feel. She took in the rough bark of a nearby tree, she could almost imagine that she was on vacation, the sun warming her skin, the lack of bugs here making it so much better than being on the mainland. She headed to where the community and health center resided, an equal distance from all five different housing areas that had been completed, each of which could accommodate fifty people. There would be so much more room for other housing sites if they got the green light. Once the island was up and running for some time, once Olivia proved that it could and would make a difference on the mainland, they would get the go-ahead to build more.

As she took in the absolute beauty all around her, she wondered if the future residents that were going to live here understood how lucky they happened to be. They were being offered this paradise. Or would they only be concerned about being able to get their daily dose of Ink for free?

Before opening the door to the community center, Olivia paused for a moment, lost in thought, remembering.

It had been Valentine's Day. She had bought a gift, a beautiful gold necklace with a diamond heart pendant surrounded by a ruby cluster. It was brilliant and shiny, breathtaking to look at. She waited for the right moment to present this precious gift, a piece of her heart really. Only the right moment never came. A phone call came from the local police station. They needed her to come down right away to pick Aria up. Again. Another special occasion ruined, yet another perfect moment gone to hell because Aria just couldn't stay clean. Olivia hated that black liquid then. Ink, that dark, sticky substance that people shot into their veins chasing whatever high they could. Her bitter thought that day was that for addicts, the high was apparently better than real life and relationships with people that loved them.

Shaking the memory off, Olivia decided to find Ameera first, to go over procedures and how she was going to handle the physicals and birth-control implementation. Walking through the glass doors that led into the health-center entrance, she saw no sign of her. Wondering where she could be, Olivia wandered the building, heading toward the community center. The halls were not plain colors like most establishments. These walls were a riot of color and action, murals running into other murals, eliciting happiness, and making you want to dance. Hearing laughter and music, Olivia adjusted and headed in the direction of the sound, seeing Ameera and Zek laughing and dancing around. Glad that she'd found them, and in such good spirits, she called out, "Well, this looks like the place to be!"

Zek waved dramatically. "Our fearless leader comes to check on us. How are you, my dear Olivia?"

"I am well. I just wanted to make sure that you were all set to go. Residents will begin arriving in about an hour. How are you?"

"Oh, I'm good. Missing my husband a little bit, but we video chat every night so I can see his handsome face. I have a list of community resources set up for everyone once they begin to arrive. I'm not sure how much they will want to do first thing, but I will make sure to keep them engaged as much as I possibly can."

"What do you have going on for the first week?"

"Lots of music on week one. Pretty much everyone likes music, right?"

"That's great, I know that I do." And turning to Ameera, Olivia asked, "How are you today? Have you gotten together with Intake to set up the physicals and birth-control implants?"

"You worry too much, Olivia. That has been set for days. You hired us because we are the best at what we do. Let us do it, *mi amor*."

Chuckling approvingly at her candor, Olivia patted Ameera on the back and replied with, "I do enjoy your honesty. Have a good first day, guys. You know how to reach me if you need me."

She walked outside, got into an orange jeep, and drove to the intake area by the docks where Gail, Dave, and Claudia were, prepping for people to arrive, going over the contracts, housing, and orientation for the new residents of Euphoria. At least this week should be easy. Everyone coming in today had volunteered to be here, choosing this new way of life. Sure, there would still be problems on the mainland, but this project should help clean up the streets enough to make a difference, and they had room to expand some more when they got the green light.

She pulled up to the intake building, which was a short walk from one of two access points on the outer edge of the island. This dock was for passenger ships, bringing regular workers and residents across the long stretch of ocean to their new home. The other access point on the far side of the island was for emergencies. The entire island setup was meant for efficiency and ease of security, making sure that no one could come or go without prior approval. The entire perimeter of the island had laser sensors set up to detect movement and would ping if something larger than a child went through. Right now, the sensors for the public dock were turned off to allow the passenger ships in without setting off alarms. Walking into the building, Olivia made her way to Dave, seeing the stress written all over his face.

Gently, she said, "Relax, Dave. Everything is in working order and looking good."

Looking at her with worry-filled eyes, he asked, "What if I didn't choose wisely when I went through all the applications? What if we fail because of some of the people that I decided to bring over and give a chance to?"

Olivia's eyes roamed the office space, catching sight of Gail and Claudia in the next room over, having an animated conversation, all smiles and laughter. Turning her attention back to Dave, she said, "You're putting far too much pressure on yourself. Claudia helped you with the initial applications and she doesn't seem to be worried about it."

"I just don't want to let you down, and I really like this job. I would hate to lose it if Euphoria doesn't work in the way that the RED and NED are expecting it to."

Nodding and understanding the concern, Olivia placed a hand on his shoulder. "I have faith in you, Dave. I'm sure that you made the right choice. Are you sure that's all that is bothering you?"

"I'm just having a rough time with Tammy. She doesn't like that I am gone so much, so she started seeing a couple of other people. I just wish she wanted to be with just me. I don't understand what's so wrong with me that I can't find someone to love me."

"Oh no, Dave! I'm sure it's not you at all. Tammy just isn't in a place where she wants an exclusive relationship. She is just having fun playing the field and living her life. Maybe it's time to move on and think about seeing someone who has the same values that you do."

"I tried that with you, Liv, but you weren't into me either."

"You cannot compare Tammy and I, Dave. I don't want a relationship of any kind with anybody. It has nothing to do with you. That is entirely on me. Now take some deep breaths and focus. I can see the ship on the horizon. Apparently, they are running early. They weren't supposed to be here for another half hour. Gail, Claudia, it's go-time. The ship is almost to port!"

After making sure that her three employees were all set and ready to go, Olivia walked down to the dock, watching the ship come into port, taking its time docking. She watched the faces of the people on board, seeing nervousness, excitement, calm, and even sadness showing in their eyes. Thankful that she didn't recognize anybody, she placed a kind smile on her face, wanting these people to know that she was here to help them adjust to island life. It took another fifteen minutes for the boat to secure itself and drop the platform for residents to make their way off the boat, most of them having just one backpack full of personal belongings. Feeling sadness drifting through her, she couldn't imagine having all of her belongings fit into one singular bag. She hoped that this place would allow for a better life for them, with a home that they wouldn't have to worry about losing.

Shaking herself from her reverie, Olivia moved back toward the building, walking with her new residents, making small talk, trying to ease their nervousness as they moved into this new chapter of their lives. One woman clutched her hands tightly together, looking around with fear evident in her eyes. Another shifted her weight back and forth from leg to leg, eyes darting from place to place. Olivia took in the sight of all these people that she was now responsible for. A man at the front of the line was constantly cracking his knuckles trying to look tough but not succeeding in the slightest. She walked with them to the waiting room for intake and saw that Gail was getting ready to take a group to the health center for physicals and birth control. Once that was complete, she would be taking them to their houses, after meeting Zek and receiving a schedule of community activities for the week. Pleased that everything was moving smoothly, Olivia headed to her personal office, which was in the building with the employee living quarters, where she could check her emails and communicate the successful first day to the RED and NED, sure that they would be pleased.

Before she could make her way out of the building, she saw Sari moving her way at a clipped pace, her face twisted with concern. A pit formed in Olivia's stomach as she realized that the only reason Sari would have left her post was if something was very wrong.

"Shit, Liv, we have a problem. I need you to come with me now." Not waiting for an acknowledgment, Sari turned and walked briskly to the door, leaving Olivia rushing to catch up.

Panic set in as Olivia raced to catch up and jump into the jeep. "What's going on, Sari? You're scaring me."

The engine revved as Sari stepped on the gas, peeling out of the parking lot. "Alarms started going off on the beach quadrant. Liv, a body washed up on shore. I've already called the Coastal Patrol and the mainland authorities. They are all enroute."

"A body? Like a human body? Sari are you serious?!?!"

23

The sheer volume of thoughts that ran through Olivia's mind in the short time that it took to drive to the quarantined area was astounding. She contemplated all the steps that would need to be taken to get a tally of the residents to find out if any were missing.

I mean someone must be missing from somewhere. There is a dead body for Christ's sake. How does this happen on day one when I have my first residents showing up to Intake? How did this happen? We don't even have anyone living here yet. Oh my god, what if it is one of my staff members?

"Earth to Olivia! Get your shit together," Sari ground out through clenched teeth. "We have to go down to the water and meet the Ocean Guard and the police."

"I'm sorry. I panicked. I think I'm alright now. How did this happen?"

"It seems that the body washed up on shore during high tide. Now that it has moved back out it left the body behind, caught on some rocks."

"Have you seen it yet? Is it one of our people?"

"Yes, I've seen it. No, I do not believe that it is one of ours."

They picked their way through the trail that led to the ocean gingerly. Both of them were preparing for what they were about to witness as they stepped out onto the shore.

The body was caught by tattered clothing on a sharp rock that was protruding from the sand. It hung at an awkward angle, the head dangling backwards, dead eyes staring, unseeing , up into the sky. Its mouth hung open and at an unnatural angle. Olivia looked closer at the oddity and realized that a piece of the man's face was missing. Her stomach lurched as she took in the swollen, misshapen body. It looked as though creatures had feasted on portions of the body, leaving pieces of flesh hanging here and there.

Olivia turned away quickly, fighting to keep her lunch down. A feeling of relief flooded her when she heard the boats pulling up. This was beyond her pay grade, and she had no idea what to do. She looked expectantly at the captain as he made his way toward her.

"Miss Titos, I presume," the captain spoke with authority.

"Yes, what can I do to help?"

"Just stand aside, ma'am. We will handle the scene now."

Glad to let someone else take the lead, Olivia wandered over to the edge of the trail, putting as much distance as she could between her and the corpse. She focused on her breathing to keep her thoughts from running wild again. A body on the shore. Breathe in four, hold four... This can't be a good omen... Breathe out four, hold four. Of all the islands for a dead body to land on it has to be mine?!?! Breathe, Olivia, just breathe. For fuck's sake, why now?!?!

A voice frightened her out of her reverie. "Miss Titos, we believe that we have identified the body as a fisherman that went missing a couple of days ago from the mainland. We have to have his family identify him for it to be official, but the guys on the crew knew him well enough to say it's him."

"Oh, I'm so sorry for their loss. What are the next steps?"

"The body will be bagged and brought to the mainland morgue."

"Is there anything that you need from me? A press release or conference?"

Clearing his throat and looking quite uncomfortable, he replied, "We have been instructed by NED to keep this under our hats and under the radar due to the opening of Euphoria today."

Shook to the core by his words, Olivia could only nod as he excused himself to wrap up the scene.

Olivia scanned the area for Sari, seeing her deep in conversation with the captain. She mulled his words over, and while she could understand the wisdom in them, a man was dead.

What did it say about the people in power at the NED that they would downplay a death to make their lives easier? A worrisome feeling began to creep through her as she contemplated the agency that she worked for and what they were willing to do to be successful in their endeavors.

There were so many questions and concerns circling Olivia's mind that it was like a colorful and chaotic whirlwind. How did a local fisherman, someone who should have known the seas and the weather patterns, end up drowning? Why had he been out fishing alone without a crew? How the hell did he end up on Euphoria of all places? None of it made any sense to Olivia. The entire situation was surreal, planting tiny seeds of suspicion in her mind.

24

The last few days since the first residents' arrival had been running smoothly with only a couple of hiccups that were quickly addressed, which pleased Olivia immensely. That is if you didn't count the body washing up on shore during the first wave of intakes. Sighing deeply, she tucked the concerns in the back of her mind and got ready to take a tour of the island with Sari and take a routine check of the security system, as well as check on the residents to make sure they were settling in alright. Olivia and her team were not there to run these people's lives, only to observe and assist where needed. It was early still, the sun barely having risen. Most would likely still be sound asleep in their tiny houses, with one bedroom, one bathroom, a living room, and an eat-in kitchen combined. Not bad for free housing.

Standing outside, waiting for Sari to come down, Olivia took in the beauty of this place, the pinks in the sky, the greens of the trees and bushes, the sand and stone, feeling the warm air on her skin, breathing it in. Her hopes and career all resided here, in this place, with these people who had chosen a life free from the angry eyes of society. The part that people didn't seem to understand about her was that she was very much against the use of drugs, especially Ink, but if she could clean the streets of her region by building this place where people were free to do as they pleased, then so be it. Raising her face to the rising sun, her dress loose and billowy in the breeze, she tried to soak in the simplicity of this moment before beginning work for the day. Just breathing, feeling, and not thinking anymore.

Someone reached for Olivia's arm, touching her softly, and Olivia screamed and jumped away, ready to run, making Sari double over with laughter while trying to apologize. Laughing still, Sari took the keys from Olivia. "I'm driving, since you are so oblivious and jumpy this morning."

Hand on her heart, Olivia nodded in agreement. "Well I wasn't expecting you to try and terrify me. What a lovely day to have a heart attack. Thanks Sari!"

Jumping into the driver's seat while dressed comfortably in shorts and a T-shirt, Sari raised an eyebrow. "Come on, Liv, get in. We have work to do." She watched Olivia struggle to climb up into the jeep with her dress on, trying not to let it ride up too high on her thighs.

Noticing the look in Sari's eyes, Olivia sighed, "Do you ever think of anything other than sex , Sari, seriously?"

"No, sweetheart, because I have to think about it enough for both of us. That's a full-time job. Now, where did you want to go first?"

"This is your tour since we are checking the security systems. I'm just along for the ride and to check out the housing areas on our way through."

They made their way around the perimeter of the island, Sari tracking wires and sensors, Olivia lost in thought, keeping an eye out for anything unusual. The day grew warmer, though the breeze managed to keep the temperature bearable. Coming into the first of three full housing areas, they saw that all seemed to be in order. Olivia paid close attention to the cleanliness of the area. According to their contracts, residents had to maintain clean living areas, especially with their use of drugs. Needles were not allowed here. They had to take the Ink in a pill or powder form. All bags had been searched upon arrival, but you never know. It was possible that someone had been able to sneak items in unobserved. Not seeing anything out of the ordinary, or anything to cause a more intense look into the area, they moved on to the next. In the second area they found a few people up and moving around, gathering around an outdoor picnic area, waving at them as they drove through. "They don't look like typical Ink users, Sari. They aren't overly thin or in need of dental work. I wonder how they ended up being approved by Dave."

"Not everyone that he approved was an Ink user. He allowed some that listed psychedelics as their need, like LSD and ecstasy."

"That wasn't the idea for Euphoria. Why would he do that? Euphoria was intended for those with hard drug addictions that don't want to get clean. People that use psychedelics are perfectly capable of functioning in everyday society. They are not part of the problem we're attempting to fix."

"Right, Liv, but you don't want to rock the boat, do you? Keep your eye on it, but don't fix it if it's not broken. They seem friendly. Maybe they will end up being an added benefit to society here. Let's keep a watch on this and make a call when things settle."

"This is the kind of fuck-up that could end this project, Sari. I will be having a word with Dave about getting these people sent back home. Period. This is not something that is up for discussion."

"It's your island, Liv. Just hear him out before you blow up on him."

"It sounds as though you are defending him. Either that or you know something that I do not. Either of those are not acceptable from my security director," Olivia said, her words icy and biting, causing Sari to visibly flinch.

Silenced on the subject, they continued their trek through the island, driving through the third area. Seeing everything in order and no one up and about this morning, they drove on to the community center. The bright colors of the center always managed to make Olivia feel more alive and raise her energy to higher levels. She jumped down out of the jeep in one fluid movement, waiting for Sari to catch up, the woman coming around the other side of the vehicle. Zek had already caught sight of them and was waving through the large glass window of the studio gym section. As she made a mental note to come down and workout later, Olivia made her way to the gym followed by Sari, who, soon after saying hello to Zek, went to go see Ameera in the health center.

Settling in beside Zek, Olivia asked, "How are things going so far? Do you have people participating in community events?"

"So far so good. I wanted to talk to you about something, so I'm glad that you stopped by this morning. I would really like to bring live bands to Euphoria, if possible, but I doubt that the powers that be would go for that."

"That is a fantastic idea, Zek, but with the difficulties that we are having with public approval, I can't see that happening. What if we hooked into the sound system and one of us could play DJ?"

"That could work! Great idea, Olivia."

"What other community-based ideas do you have planned so far?"

"I was thinking about doing some class-type gatherings, but I'm not sure if the residents would be interested or not. What do you think?"

"I think that's a great idea. I hope that they will join. Something to get everyone mingling would be nice."

"I like that idea, get everyone mingling. They could almost walk to the different communities together if they wanted."

"There is a shuttle that runs between communities three times per day if they want to go visit friends. We don't want anyone feeling separated or segregated."

"I will plan some classes then. I hope to keep our residents active within their communities as much as possible."

"You are a true gem, Zek! How is your husband handling you being away for such long periods of time?"

"He's alright with it. His job keeps him terribly busy, always on the go. I am so proud of the things that he is accomplishing within his world. Right now, he is advocating for underprivileged workers who do not have any health-care benefits. Tom has been helping them fill out government applications for health insurance and he audits businesses to make sure that they are offering appropriate insurance based on government regulations. He says it seems like a never-ending issue, one that may not be resolved in his lifetime, but he is dedicated to trying to make some headway."

"It sounds like he's really trying to make a difference for people where it really matters, Zek. That's great. Only a few more days and we will be heading back to the mainland, so you can spend some time with him soon."

"Yes ma'am, I am looking forward to that. He said he has a couple of fun-filled days planned for us when I get home. He is taking the two days off as well, so we can spend all of it together."

"It sounds like you have a couple of great days coming, my friend," Olivia said as she turned to head toward the health center where Sari was with Ameera. Walking down the hallway, which was a riot of color, Olivia thought of her crew and how amazing each one of them were in their own way, and how lucky she was to find them for this island and her dream. Even with Dave's huge mistake, she was still thankful for him and his huge heart. She just knew that together they could make a difference in the world, helping and healing it.

She was in a bit of a daze when she made it to the health office, startled out of her daydream by the sight of Sari and Ameera entwined, kissing deeply, bodies pressed tight together, Ameera up on the counter with Sari between her legs, a moan escaping Ameera's mouth, causing Sari to press closer, deepening the kiss, hands working Ameera's supple, curvaceous body. Clearing her throat loudly, Olivia hoped to startle them out of their passionate embrace, but neither of them seemed to hear it. Now irritated because it was on the clock and on her time, she slammed her hand down on the countertop near the entrance to the center, knowing that they wouldn't be able to ignore that. Jumping apart, both Sari and Ameera looked toward her with guilty expressions on their faces.

She frowned at them. "What the two of you choose to do on your time is up to you, but when you are on the clock, I expect you to act in a professional manner. I do not care if there are clients here or not, you are on the clock. You need to uphold a certain standard! You understand that I have to document this now, right? What the hell were the two of you thinking? We are already in the spotlight getting this island up and running with so many people just waiting for us to fail. I've already been under scrutiny for choosing people close to me as supervisors. Now I walk in to see this happening. I am so disappointed in both of you."

They separated, Sari mumbling something about going out to wait in the jeep for Olivia. Ameera looked at Olivia sheepishly. "I am sorry for that. It's been a few weeks since I have been intimate with someone, and well, Sari is very enticing. Not that it is an excuse. I just want to be honest with you."

"You realize that this entire island is covered with security cameras? They're everywhere, including right there." Olivia pointed up just above their heads to a small camera, poking out of the ceiling and covered with blue bulletproof glass.

"It was just some kissing. Inappropriate, yes, but nothing more. I will not make that mistake again, Olivia. I promise you."

"Not to mention that it could have been someone else walking in and seeing that encounter. I can't even fathom the disaster that could have come from your simple kissing! Ameera, I would have had no choice but to fire you both if that had happened!"

"I am not sure what more I can say, Olivia. I understand, and it will not happen again."

"I have no doubt. Now, the reason that I came over. How has everyone reacted so far to the birth control and physicals?"

"I haven't had any complaints and the nurse on staff had only good reports. This group was voluntary, though. If there are going to be issues, I imagine that they will come from the ones being sent over forcibly."

"That is what I was thinking as well. Let's hope that they see this as the opportunity that it is for them. With any luck, they will adjust quickly and embrace life here. Really, it's far better for them here than over on the mainland. If you need anything, just give me a call.

I need your reports sometime within the next two days so I can get them compiled and emailed to the RED."

"I will get right on that. They are almost finished now, anyway. I believe Dave was asking if you were going to be around today. He said something about checking on some names with you."

"Thanks for letting me know. That's where we are headed next."

Waving distractedly, Ameera was already sitting at her desk, starting her work for the day. So much of what they needed to do was report after report for the directors. Wishing that she could spend more time actively involved like some of her regular crew members, Olivia made a mental note to figure out how to streamline the report system over the next few weeks. Walking out of the building into the sunshine, she hopped up in the jeep, and giving Sari a withering look, she motioned that she was ready to go.

"Liv, don't be mad at me. I'm sorry. We started talking about the old days and then it just happened. I know it was foolish and not at all appropriate, but she and I are both highly sexual creatures, and it can be tough not having that connection with someone here. It's not like I can go to the bar and pick someone up for the evening."

Turning to face Sari, Olivia looked her dead in the eyes. "That is not an excuse. Not even close. Wait until after work hours and invite her to your condo or go to hers. Hell, since you have such a high sex drive, you could even go condo hopping and change it up every night. Just don't do it on my time, or work time again. This project means more to me than you know. I will not have some bullshit thing like sex fuck it all up when it is still in its infancy!"

"Being a bit harsh, don't you think? Geez, Olivia, people make mistakes. We said it won't happen again, and my bet is this isn't the only time you will have an issue with sex here. We are on an island, with nobody else around. Most people are sex-driven. Don't be blind about it just because you have issues with sex yourself."

Feeling the sting of Sari's words, Olivia snapped. "How dare you use things that I've told you in confidence against me when you are the one that fucked up!"

"I'm sorry, Liv," Sari whispered as shame moved over her face.

Eyes shining with unshed tears, Olivia said thickly, "Stop here at this building. This is where Dave is working today, and I believe he has Claudia here with him as well."

She jumped out of the jeep without a backward glance as Sari was trying to reach for her. Back ramrod straight as she entered the building, Olivia found Dave and Claudia with stacks of paperwork in front of them, both sitting at one desk pouring through the pages of court-ordered residents that would arrive the following week. They were so intent on what they were doing that they didn't even notice that Olivia had walked into the office. A stack of papers suddenly fell to the floor, scattering everywhere. Olivia said gently, "You both seemed buried under the workload. If you need assistance, I can get Gail over here to help."

Claudia began picking up the papers scattered all about the floor, and Dave looked up from his work with a half-smile. "That would be really great. There is so much to do, and I really want to be able to go home this upcoming weekend. That won't happen unless we get some help."

"Of course! Why didn't you ask me for someone before this? Gail has her area well settled and she can always cross over and give you guys a hand when you need it. The only time she won't have time is when we get new residents in."

"I don't want you to think that I can't do my job, Liv. I know it sounds prideful, but that's not what I meant. I want you to know that you hired the right person. I am good at this. I just wasn't expecting the minute details and lack of information with the court-ordered cases. We've had to make so many phone calls and send emails trying to gather all the information we need to get them entered in the system, and some people aren't exactly cooperating."

Finding her voice and speaking up, Claudia added, "I had one gentleman tell me that he felt that the individual that I was calling about should be rotting in jail, not being sent to a vacation island, and therefore he would not give me the information that I requested. I mentioned that he would be going against the RED protocol if he did not comply, and he told me that the RED can suck his balls."

Olivia had known that there would be resistance to Euphoria, but to be so blatantly disrespectful to not only Claudia, but to the RED, shocked and upset Olivia greatly. "I would like his name, and the file that you were trying to complete please. I will handle that case personally, and I will make sure to let the RED know what he wishes for them to do. There is no reason to be so rude, especially to you when you are simply trying to do your job. If anything like that happens again, I ask that you inform me immediately." Taking the file from Claudia, she said, "Gail will be here in an hour to give you a hand."

Olivia turned to Dave, motioning him to walk with her. "I need a word with you please."

Concern flitted across his face as he followed. "What's up, Liv?"

"Speaking of doing your job, Dave, I noticed that there is a large group of residents that are not Ink users. It seems that you let an entire community of hallucinogen users in. You know that is not the purpose of this project. This could break us. We need to figure out how to send them back without looking incompetent."

"They can't go back, Liv. They are a permanent part of Euphoria."

Taken aback, Olivia's voice rose slightly. "Who are you to make a decision like that? Find a way to send them home, Dave."

"No. I can't. You aren't the only one that makes decisions here, Liv. This order came from above you. Sorry, but the request came directly from the NED."

"What? Why wasn't I informed of this? And who was the official that requested all of this?"

"I was told that it was to be kept quiet so that the public didn't protest even more. I wasn't allowed to share it with anyone. The only reason that I'm even discussing it now is because I was given the okay to talk to you if you were to come to me. The order came from the NED. No specific director was attached to it."

Olivia stared at Dave in stunned silence, processing all that he'd said to her.

"I'm sorry, Liv. You know that I would never keep anything from you, but I didn't have a choice."

"We all have choices, Dave. You made yours. I will let you get back to it."

Finding Sari in the office with Claudia, Olivia said brusquely, "Let's go. I need to get to my office and take care of things."

Going over all that had occurred today, Olivia felt the weight that was sitting squarely on her shoulders. The success, or failure, of Euphoria was not something shared amongst her and her friends as she had initially imagined. This was hers and hers alone. She felt a sense of loneliness settle in. Her hair blew in the wind as they drove back to the central office. Olivia was lost in thought, compiling lists of emails to send, reports to complete, complaints to be handled.

"You know you can't fix the world, Olivia."

Olivia looked at Sari and saw her watching her with passionate eyes. "I might know that, Sari, but that doesn't mean that I'm not going to try. I won't let anyone try to shoot down what I am building here. No one is going to get in my way. Give it a year, then they'll see how great an idea this is. When people can walk to their cars in the dark and not worry about being mugged or walk in their yards without finding dirty needles from an addict, then they will see."

"I hope that you're right, Liv. I staked my career on the promise that I made to help you here."

"I am right, and so have I. More so than anybody else here. If this fails, you can go find another job in the field. I won't be able to find work in any agency again. That bullshit that you pulled earlier could have messed this up for all of us."

25

It was time to head home for a few days. She required all staff to take a few days away from Euphoria even if they wanted to stay on the island just so they could decompress from the job. Being away from work was important, even if work did seem like a paradise most of the time. Just because she was the boss didn't mean that she wasn't also required to follow protocol, so even though she had a bit of anxiety about heading home, she had to set an example.

Feeling the lift of the helicopter, excitement for the next couple of days coursed through her alongside a slight twinge of worry as she wondered if she was going to see Joe and Hannah together. Wanting to get her mind off that, Olivia opened her eyes and looked out at the deep blue sea, taking in the beauty of the water all around them, surprised to see land not far off in the distance.

She hadn't realized that she had been lost in her daydream for so long, wondering if she may have fallen into a light sleep on the way over. The land got closer and closer, and upon seeing the shuttle waiting in the field for its passengers, she began to get even more excited, although she was also curious about the car parked next to the shuttle. "Does anybody recognize that car there?" she asked the group.

Smiling wide, Zek replied, "That's my husband Tom. He said he just couldn't wait to see me, so he wanted to pick me up at the base. I hope that's alright with you. The security personnel didn't seem to mind."

"That's perfectly fine and so sweet of him. I am sure that the two of you will have a wonderful weekend," she replied while looking out the window at the man that was leaning against the sleek blue car and waving excitedly, smiling as though he could hardly contain himself. A tiny smidge of envy crept over Olivia, seeing Zek and Tom's display of absolute adoration for one another, the two of them so obviously in love.

As the helicopter landed, she became a little concerned that Zek might just jump the last few feet to the ground to get to his husband faster. She moved to the side to make room for him to hop down out of the helicopter as soon as they got the go-ahead from the pilot, afraid that she might get run over. Olivia watched with a frown as Zek embraced Tom tightly, kissing him as they began to talk animatedly. As she walked to the shuttle hoping to avoid them, Zek brought his husband up to her, introducing him, pride flowing out of him each time he looked toward his mate. Olivia shook his hand, a tight smile on her face. "It is a pleasure to meet you, Tom. Zek tells me that you do some amazing things for the underprivileged. That is a calling of the highest order."

"Likewise, Miss Tito. It is a huge bull that you have grabbed by the horns by battling the issue of Ink and attempting to make our streets safer. I hope that it all works out as planned for you! Zek seems quite happy with his job. I would love to see it become permanent."

"I am sure that it will continue to be funded by the RED. It is sure to show at least a small margin of improvement in some smaller cities in the near future. Once we have the go-ahead to build more housing communities, we can take on more residents and make an even greater difference, hopefully in the larger cities as well."

"I wish you much luck in that endeavor, Miss Titos. Have a wonderful weekend! I have some surprises for my handsome Zek. Until next time," Tom said, taking her hand and kissing the back of it as though she were royalty, making her smile and blush.

"Take care, guys, I will see you back here first thing Monday morning at 6 a.m.," Olivia said curtly. Sliding into the shuttle beside Gail and Dave, she asked if they had any big plans for the weekend.

Dave looked a bit worried, shrugging his shoulders slightly. "I was hoping to take Tammy out somewhere, but she hasn't really responded well to any of my suggestions."

Gail replied, "My husband and I are going to see some family and just enjoy downtime together. I hope that your girlfriend comes around to your ideas, Dave. I'm sure they are good ones."

Dave tried to smile and agree, but it was half-hearted, worry showing all over his handsome face and downcast eyes. Looking out the window, away from the ladies, he made it clear that he didn't really want to talk about it anymore, sadness shining in his ice blue eyes. What sounded like a gunshot made everyone in the shuttle jump a mile. Olivia looked out her window and saw a crowd of people, protestors, surrounding the gates and lined up down the fence on both sides. This was unlike the crowd at the press conference. This group was angrier and throwing all manner of items at the shuttle, screaming profanities and threats. The sound came again, but this time they watched a security guard fall to the ground. Chaos erupted as another guard dove into the crowd to apprehend the shooter while others gathered around the fallen man.

"Oh my god," Dave cried, "that man was shot!"

The driver spoke up. "Don't worry. He should be fine. They have bulletproof gear."

Olivia, shaken to the core commented, "What? That doesn't make this okay. None of this okay!"

Pulling himself together to comfort Olivia, Dave reassured her. "They are trained and know how to handle these things, right? I'm sure they will get everything under control."

"A man just got shot, Dave! I had no idea that it had gotten his bad."

The driver pointed out that the man that had been shot was getting up. Though clutching his chest in pain, at least he was able to make his way to the medical transport on his own.

Olivia pulled out her phone and called Headquarters immediately only to be sent to voicemail. Highly agitated, she questioned the shuttle driver. "Has it been like this every day?"

"No, only on days that people are being transported."

"Well how the hell do these people know when that is happening?"

"Not sure, Miss Titos. I can only tell ya what I see when it happens."

"Why hasn't anyone reported this to me?" Olivia questioned irritably.

"Not sure, ma'am," the driver replied, keeping his eyes on the crowd.

They made their way slowly through the rowdy crowd, trash continuing to be thrown at the van. The stress that Olivia was hoping to leave behind on Euphoria had followed her home. She sighed heavily, tears beginning to well up behind her eyes. She fought down the lump in her throat, not wanting her colleagues to see her become emotional.

She said reassuringly to them, "I will get to the bottom of this tomorrow and make sure that we have a stronger officer presence when we are coming and going from now on." The rest of the group nodded and murmured agreeably, though fear was etched on their faces.

As the shuttle got closer to her house, Olivia began to get more and more excited about being in her own space, even if she did have to share it with Hannah for the time being. That tiny blonde was a bundle of energy, but she was also very sweet and exceptional with the cats, making sure that they always had the proper amount of playtime. She kept them well fed and clean, not to mention how well she kept the house. Hannah was a great roommate and a good person. The only blemish was that Joe had taken such an interest in her, not allowing Olivia to see if she could grow feelings for him or not. She hoped that she wouldn't have to see him while she was home, but as the shuttle pulled up out front of her house, she saw Joe's car parked next to hers. Thanking the driver, she got her bag and headed for the front door, and finding it unlocked, she walked in, not sure what to expect.

"Oh, thank heavens you're home!" Hannah exclaimed, her eyes wide and filled with worry. She was breathing heavily as she rushed over to embrace her. "I had to call Joe because I was so worried about Molly. She was making these weird noises and crouching funny, I was so afraid that she was in pain."

"What? Where is she? What's wrong with her?" Olivia asked, moving farther into the living room, seeing Joe sitting on the floor holding Molly in his lap.

Smiling up at Olivia hesitantly, Joe said soothingly, "Don't worry, Olivia. She is fine. Hannah wasn't aware of how cats act when they are in heat. The crouching that she is talking about is the reproductive position. No worries at all. Hannah said that you have an appointment for Molly to be spayed tomorrow morning anyway. Just a heads-up that they might charge a bit more since she is currently in heat, but they can still do the procedure."

"Oh, thank goodness! I don't know what I would do if something were wrong with her. If you will excuse me, I need to get my bags situated." Reaching for Molly, Olivia carried her into the bedroom and closed the door.

Sinking down onto the bed and cuddling her precious Molly, she waited to feel some sort of emotion that would tell her that she was wrong to let go of Joe, but none came. As she stroked Molly's soft black fur, the others came racing up, jumping on the bed, followed more slowly by Max, who seemed to sit back, content to watch his family interact with his person. Olivia loved on and cuddled them all.

She heard hushed voices coming from the other room. She attempted to tune them out and just focus on the cats, but that seemed to be easier said than done. She could tell that they had now moved into Hannah's room, and she still heard their voices, with long moments of silence between.

Olivia remembered his kisses and didn't want to keep playing the possibilities over and over again in her mind, so she threw on a bikini, grabbed a towel, and headed out to the pool to go for a swim. She could hear a soft moan as she entered the hallway. She shut her bedroom door loudly and moved quickly toward the other end of the house.

Looking out over her backyard, she took in the large inground pool with its stone facades and tropical plants, the concrete surrounding it made to look like a sandy beach, her incredibly comfortable lounge chairs, the waterfall fountain at the far end of the pool. All of this she had worked so hard for, creating a sacred space for herself and Aria. A place that they would never have to take a vacation from, a place that they could sink into and relax, letting their love flourish. Then that was torn from her when Aria decided to chase a story and got in too deep. Now this was hers alone to cherish, her place of solitude and peace. Which she was usually okay with, but knowing that Hannah was locked in a passionate embrace in one of the guest rooms with a man that Olivia herself had wrongly thought may have been able to awaken her desires, she wished that she had someone to share all of this with.

Moving to dive into the heated pool, she stood poised, seeing her reflection in the water, beautiful, strong, even sexy, many people had said, but if that were so, then how wasn't she enough to keep her fiancée from choosing something else over her? She was irritated already with the bathing suit that she'd put on for proper decorum simply because Joe was there. Screw it. She decided that this was her house, and he had seen her naked anyway, so she ripped the bikini off and threw it aside.

She dove into the deep warm water, feeling it caress her skin as she glided through, beginning her warmup lap. She hadn't been working out as much as usual, busy with getting the island up and running. Now that she had time to herself, it was going to be a priority, and the goal right now was fifty laps. Settling into a steady pace, she cut through the water, not thinking about anything except her strokes, focusing fully on her form. She loved the way her body felt as she demanded it to perform well. Her muscles grew tired around lap forty, but she kept pushing. Never one to quit, she dug in and forced herself to finish out the last ten laps before turning over and floating on her back, looking up at the clear blue sky.

She lost track of time lying in the sun naked, eyes closed, happy to finally be home. The sound of someone clearing their throat pulled her from her reverie. She opened her eyes slightly to see Hannah standing next to her, Joe a little way back trying not to look at Olivia's naked body unsuccessfully.

"I didn't mean to bother you, Olivia, but your phone was blowing up. It just kept ringing and dinging, so I figured that it must be an emergency or something. I brought it out here for you." Handing her the phone, Hannah turned back to the house and saw Joe checking Olivia out. He looked at Hannah with a guilty expression and shrugged as if to say, *what do you expect?*

Concerned, Olivia checked her phone and saw a bunch of missed calls from Dave, and one from Sari, but no voicemails. She opened her text messages and saw one from Sari telling her to check on Dave, and there were at least a dozen from Dave himself, asking if she was around, saying he was sorry for bothering her and to please get back to him when she could. She sent him a text. *Are you alright?* While she waited for a reply, her worry grew as each minute passed without an answer.

Not able to sit any longer, she got up to go put some clothes on, thinking that if he didn't respond by the time she was done, she was going over to his place. She walked by Hannah and Joe in the kitchen who were engaged in a heated discussion when her phone finally dinged. With a sigh of relief, she checked it as she continued to her bedroom. Seeing that it was from Dave, she opened it quickly. All it said was, *Can I come by? I need to talk*, to which she replied, *of course.* As an added thought, she also replied, *I will call in an order from our favorite Chinese food place and pay if you pick it up*, knowing that food always made him feel better.

Sure, was all he said.

26

Now clothed in a pretty blue sundress, the gauzy material floating around her body. Olivia headed to the kitchen to let Hannah know that Dave would be coming over and that they might need some space depending on how he was feeling. Upon stepping into the kitchen, her eyes landed on Hannah, head resting against Joe's shoulder, both of them looking out the back window, having a quiet conversation, fingers entwined, looking so perfect together. She felt like she was seeing a future picture of what they would look like in their own kitchen one day, but this one was hers and her friend needed her. Clearing her throat to make them aware of her presence, she stepped fully into the room. Hannah jumped away from Joe with a guilty look on her face.

"Hannah, seriously, it's fine. I know that the two of you are together. I really don't care. He and I shared some good conversations and a few kisses. It was nothing. Neither of us had feelings for the other. We just enjoyed each other's company."

Looking from Olivia to Hannah uncomfortably, Joe said, "She's right. It really wasn't anything. I've said the same to you before."

"Alright. I get it, but I still feel funny about it sometimes," Hannah said. "Did you need something, Olivia, or would you just like us to stop being so much in your space?"

"I just wanted to let you know that my friend Dave will be coming over shortly with Chinese. I'm not sure what kind of mood he will be in, so I may need some space. You don't have to leave by any means, I just might need some room, that's all."

"Okay, no problem. Joe was just asking me where I wanted to go to eat. I was thinking of staying over at his place tonight anyway, so you had some time alone. I know how you like to be by yourself."

"That would be lovely, Hannah, thank you. I could use some solitude. I hope you guys have a wonderful evening." She checked her refrigerator to make sure a bottle of wine was chilled for dinner and walked out onto the back porch to wait for Dave to arrive.

She heard Dave pull in shortly after the others had left. She went to get a couple of glasses, wine, and an ice bucket. Olivia wondered just how upset he was going to be, trying to decide if alcohol might not be the best idea, but decided to play it by ear. Dave was walking through the back gate as she was making her way back out onto the porch. She set the glasses and the ice bucket with wine down, moving to give Dave a hug, seeing that his eyes were bloodshot, as though he had been crying. Heart sinking to her feet, Olivia realized that this might be what she was fearing. Maybe he and Tammy had broken up. He held Olivia tight for a moment, and she let him. She could feel the shaking in his body, knowing that he was struggling to keep it together and didn't want her to visibly see that struggle.

Releasing her slowly, Dave turned away from her and sat in one of the single chairs at the tea table. Olivia followed and sat with him, not saying anything. She was simply ready to listen. The silence stretched out as she poured them each a glass of wine, handing it to him and slowly sipping from her glass. He swallowed the contents of the glass in one swig and held his glass out for more. Olivia obliged and poured more from the bottle into his glass, which he again finished in one gulp. Sighing, she stood and walked to the kitchen, getting the rocks glasses and a bottle of whisky. She wasn't letting him go anywhere tonight, not feeling this way. Setting the glasses and bottle on the table, she said, "Give me your keys. You can stay in the other guest room tonight. I won't take no for an answer because I am not having you alone like this."

He handed her the keys without a word, and she put them away where he wouldn't be able to find them. Feeling better now that she knew he would stay without a problem, she returned to the back porch. She watched him swirl the whiskey around, following the liquid as it rose and fell along the sides of the glass. He seemed to hope that he could drown in the mini whirlpool made by the brown sea in his glass. She waited what seemed like ages for Dave to speak and tell her what had him so tied up inside. Even though she already knew it had something to do with Tammy, she said nothing, allowing him space and time. As he swallowed more whiskey, the effects of the alcohol began to become evident in his eyes and voice.

He looked into Olivia's eyes and slurred slightly when he spoke. "What is so wrong with me that no one wants to stay?"

"Oh honey, you can't blame all of this on yourself," she said, reaching out and placing her hand over his.

"I should have known better. She told me that she didn't want to commit. She wanted to see other people. But I wasn't prepared for this. I wasn't prepared for how much it would hurt. I wish she had just said that she didn't want to see me anymore, instead of inviting me over tonight."

Not sure what to say at this point, Olivia waited for him to continue. She drank slowly from her glass, feeling the burn of the liquor as it flowed down her throat, a warm pool of fire in her stomach.

"I had the perfect dinner planned. It was going to be romantic, candlelit, all her favorite foods." He sighed and placed his face in his hands. "She said to come by her place first. She had something that she wanted to do before dinner. So, I went. She didn't answer the door when I knocked, so I let myself in because it wasn't locked."

Shaking his head as if to tell the past version of himself, no, don't go in there, he downed another portion of his glass. "I could hear her calling me from the back of the apartment. It sounded strange, like there was something going on, but I brushed it off and walked back to her room," he said, holding the glass up for yet another refill.

"Maybe you should slow down a little, sweetie. You won't even be able to tell me the entire story if you keep drinking this fast," Olivia suggested gently.

Dave shrugged. "I pushed open her bedroom door. I couldn't believe what I saw. I'm not sure that I still believe it. It was like something that you would see in a shitty B-rated porn flick. There she was, riding some guy in the middle of her bed, and she just smiled at me, motioning for me to join. Like, what the fuck did I just walk into? I just stood there and stared for a bit. Watching her fuck another guy. I didn't know what the hell to do. Then she said that she wanted me to fulfill her fantasy of getting caught cheating and then me joining in."

Tears welled up in his eyes, his voice catching. "But I didn't like what I saw, Liv. I didn't like it or want anything to do with it. Why does she need so many people to fulfill her needs? Why am I not enough for her? I can't get that image of her out of my head, bouncing up and down on his dick. Smiling at me like she was giving me some sort of gift, instead of ripping my heart out and shredding it on the floor."

Stunned into silence, trying hard not to flash back to her own memories, Olivia refilled both of their glasses again after slamming back what was left in hers. "It has nothing to do with you not being enough or good enough, Dave. That has no bearing on your personal value. I know it's hard to fathom, but I really can relate. I understand what you are going through right now. I am so sorry that you are hurting. What she has done and continues to do to you is awful. She knows that you care for her deeply and yet she keeps up her games. It's disgusting really. It might be time to walk away from that dumpster fire before you get burned anymore."

"The whiskey is helping to make me numb. Thanks. Not sure if I believe all the stuff about me being good enough but hey, who cares, right? Tammy surely doesn't if she can fuck random people every night."

"Dave, what can I do to help?" Olivia asked, desperate to help ease his pain, having been in a similar position before.

"Just keep the liquor coming until I pass out or die, then I won't see her like that in my head anymore," Dave slurred heavily. "I mean yeah, we did a lot of playing around with other people, but it was always together, something that we had discussed first. Even when she wanted to be with another guy, we did it together, I let her have her fun and play out her fantasies. Never something like this, where I had no clue. I wonder how many times she has been with other people without me knowing about it."

"You aren't going to die. I would never let that happen. Do you want to go inside and eat that Chinese that you brought over? It would soak up some of the alcohol," she said, reaching for his hand to pull him up, but instead he pulled her onto his lap.

"Please just hold me a minute, Liv," he said, starting to sob, face buried in her chest, tears flowing freely, his body shaking with the force of the emotion pouring from his heart. Olivia held on tight, tears falling down her face as she shared in his pain. She leaned her head in, resting it on his while stroking his back and murmuring that everything would be alright. After a short time, the body-wracking sobs slowed down and began to subside, leaving Dave clearly feeling raw and embarrassed. Letting go of Olivia, he looked down at the ground.

Reaching under his chin, Olivia turned his face up so that he was looking directly at her, their faces close together. "Never think that you aren't good enough. Never feel embarrassed by sharing emotion with me." Wrapping her arms tight around his body, she leaned in and kissed him on the cheek before she rose up off of his lap and moved toward the kitchen door. "I'll get forks. We can eat out here."

Looking out through the window at him while getting silverware, she wished that she could take away the pain. She felt so bad because she knew exactly how he felt... A flash of brown hair tangled in a beefy fist entered her mind before she could shut it down, and she almost dropped the silverware at the sudden stab of pain in her heart. She too wondered what was so wrong with her that she hadn't been able to keep the woman that she loved happy. Pulling out her last bottle of whiskey, she moved back outside, filling glasses and sticking forks in Chinese food cartons. "Screw plates, we can eat out of the box," she said, winking at Dave with a bright smile on her face, trying to make both of them feel better. Nudging a carton toward him, she convinced him to eat now that he needed to get food in his system. She reached for the chicken and stabbed a piece of it, eating it hungrily. There were no words between them now, just silence, the two of them taking refuge in each other's company.

Olivia made quick work of clearing away the containers, silverware, and napkins when they finished their meal. Looking out the window as she put everything away, she saw Dave move over to the love seat, bottle and glasses held tightly in his hand. As she came back out onto the porch he patted the seat next to him, holding up a full glass for her. Sitting on the edge of the cushion, Olivia accepted the glass from Dave as he raised his glass and said, "To real friends, good drink, and good food."

Raising her glass and sipping from it, Olivia placed her hand on Dave's in a comforting gesture, looked down and wondering what else had happened in his life for him to feel unworthy. She stared out into her backyard, silently thankful for all that she had and the lack of such insane drama in her life. Suddenly, Dave's phone started going off, and notification after notification pinged off. He looked to see who it was and took a long pull from the glass, emptying it again. He poured himself another glass before bracing himself and opening the messages. Olivia watched him with curious eyes, waiting for him to tell her if it indeed was Tammy, and if so, what she had to say.

After a few moments, another long drink from the glass, and a quick text sent back, he turned to her, sadness taking up permanent residence in his ice blue eyes. "I just can't do it anymore with her. She wants to make all these fantasies happen before she settles down, but I just can't do it. I don't want to be with other women with her or see her with other guys. All of this feels like a bad movie that never ends. I don't even think that it's about her fantasies anymore, even though she says that it is. I think she just enjoys living this way. It's not how I want to live my life. I don't need this crazy sex to make me happy. I just want a strong relationship, a happy home, vacations, and maybe a family eventually. Is that so awful?"

"There is nothing awful about that, Dave. Don't give up on your dream. You just have to wait for the right woman to come along. Unfortunately, I think that you are right about Tammy. It's time to walk away. She is proving that she isn't a good person. She knows how you feel, and she doesn't seem to care. It's bullshit, Dave. You deserve someone way better than her."

"When I walked out of her apartment earlier, I told her that I was done. I refused to play a part in her sick game. But it completely destroyed me in the process. How do I even look at another woman again without seeing all of that playing in my mind?"

"I'm really not sure. I still have issues from my experience, so I can't give you advice on that. I wish I could, but I can't. You just have to give yourself time and be patient."

"Jesus, I don't know why she keeps blowing up my phone. It's not like she has a lack of options in partners. She wants to know why I've been here for so long. She is jealous of you. She always thinks that I am trying to sleep with you. She's not wrong you know."

"That was in the past, Dave, and it'll never happen. We've discussed this."

"She keeps asking me to come back so we can talk this through. I told her that there is no talking it through, that it is over. But no matter how many times I say it's done, she won't listen." He drained his glass, looking for more. Upon seeing that the bottle was empty, he took Olivia's glass and finished it in one gulp, swaying in his seat.

"Come on, Dave, let's get you to bed. You are quite drunk, and I have no more liquor in the house. You need to sleep this off. I'm betting you'll feel like shit in the morning," she said as she took his hand

and pulled him up from the love seat. He was very unsteady on his feet, so Olivia guided him to the guest room, taking his shoes off for him. She peeled his shirt, pants, and socks off, leaving only his boxer briefs on. She pulled back the covers and maneuvered him in between the sheets, getting him settled in for sleep. She tried to leave the room, but he held on to her hand, pulling her back to the bed.

"Please stay," he slurred drunkenly. "I don't want to be alone right now."

"I know you don't want to be alone, but it would probably be best," Olivia said, pulling the covers over him. "I will be right across the hall if you need me." He nodded sadly and rolled over in the bed. She listened to his breathing deepen and even out. She watched him sleep for a bit, wondering again what his story was, the whole story from his past. Her entire group of friends was close, but they rarely spoke of their histories. She wondered what in his life had caused him to not only want the dream life so badly, but to also allow a woman to take such advantage of him in every way. Once she was sure that slipping out of the room would not wake him, she crept out, looking over her shoulder at him as she walked out the door. She knew that she would never ask about his past, so she didn't have to tell him about hers.

27

She didn't typically get nervous over new situations, but bringing the fifty court-ordered cases onto the island today had her tied up tight. So far, everyone, the employees and the residents, had made the choice to be here one way or another. These new residents, however, had not been given a choice. They were being sent here for different lengths of time based on their offenses, instead of going to a local jail. She wasn't sure how they would react to being placed here, or how they would interact with the current residents.

She was hoping for a smooth transition, but she knew something was bound to happen, which was why they had ramped up security. She needed this to work for the island to be fully accepted as part of the solution to the drug epidemic that was ravaging the nation. With the constant picketing and protests about Euphoria, she had major concerns about this next portion of the plan being implemented. If something were to go wrong the entire project could go sideways.

Another concern that had been sitting in the back of Olivia's mind was Dave. Specifically, his mental and emotional well-being. He had taken the breakup with Tammy extremely hard, drinking every night and keeping to himself. He still did his job and was up to the task in that area completely, but she could see that he was suffering. As a friend and employer, she was worried, especially about this new shake-up today. He was one of the first people that the new residents would see, so his impression on them would make a difference, and his observation of them was important feedback for her.

Euphoria was growing and she wanted to make sure that it stayed that way. No major bumps in the road right now would be beneficial to all of them.

Olivia had received word that the RED was poised to approve her request to build more housing on the island since it was going so well. That was of course contingent on the court-mandated section working as expected.

The plan was to add three additional housing areas, meaning that they would be able to house two hundred individuals, keeping the majority of residents voluntary, with only twenty-five percent of the residents being court mandated. If the island continued to work and benefit the people on the mainland and the people in power, she knew that they would be able to keep running the island.

She had no desire to go back to a tiny office cubicle, having to walk city street after city street, evaluating and reporting on how bad the drug epidemic was in the area. Now she was finally able to make a difference, not only for the people that wanted the drugs off the streets, but also for the addicts that had no desire to get clean. For the ones that knew what they were choosing and wanted their own safe space, Euphoria was a dream come true. It was a win-win situation. She just wished that everyone could see that.

She had been tracking the rates of incidents on the mainland and reporting on social media the positive impact that Euphoria was having. The declining numbers weren't astronomical yet but there was a clear indication that the project was proving to be successful. The data was clear, and numbers didn't lie, so the public-relations team had backed her idea. She was scheduled to speak at another press conference next month, once this group of residents had settled in, to relay the success of the operation that they had seen so far to the nation.

Smoothing her skirt, Olivia headed downstairs to get a ride over to the docks so she could welcome her new residents. She wondered if the skirt and shirt were too much for today, but she didn't have time to change anyway. The ride over was uneventful, the people keeping mainly to their housing areas. She did wish that they would use the community facilities more. She was sure they just hadn't found the right activities to get them interested yet, though Zek sure was trying his best. They were going to have a night-out activity in a week, hooking into the PA system and playing music in the community center. That should draw some of the residents out of their homes.

Climbing down out of the jeep, Olivia fixed her skirt again. The silky blue material blew about in the breeze, her white top tucked in. Looking chic and professional, she felt that she looked her best, but worried that it was too much for welcoming the newest group coming off the boat. Shaking the worry off, she headed inside to check in with Dave and Claudia and make sure they had everything they may need. Waving to them as she walked in, she noticed that Dave was looking unhappy as usual, though Claudia looked great. Being on the island had been good for her, building her confidence and giving her a sun-kissed glow.

"Hey guys, are you all set for the incoming group?" Olivia asked. "Is there anything that you need or that I can do for you?"

Claudia smiled brilliantly. "No, I'm fairly sure we are all set here. You look gorgeous today, Olivia!"

"Thank you, Claudia. I was just thinking about how being on the island seems to agree with you. You have a beautiful glow."

Hearing this, Claudia smiled even bigger. "I do love it here. Even though it is technically work, I have never been happier. I am so thankful that you gave me this opportunity!"

"I am happy that you accepted. You have been an integral part of this team. Right, Dave?"

Looking up with sad eyes, he said, "I couldn't do it without her here, especially now."

"I hate that I have to be your boss, instead of your friend right now," Olivia said, "but today could potentially be difficult. I need you on your A game. Is there anything that I can do to help you with that?"

Looking back and forth between Olivia and Claudia, Dave just shook his head. "Nah, I will make more of an effort to handle things, Liv. I won't let you down. Heads up, I can see the ship coming into port. Let's hope they look at this like a vacation, instead of a prison."

Butterflies filled Olivia's stomach with nervous energy as she made her way out the door and down to the docks to greet her new residents. As she was walking down the ramp, a noise to her right drew her attention. Glancing over, she saw a small group of residents from the psychedelic area had gathered with a welcome sign.

Smiling gratefully at them, she waved, hoping that this would help dull the culture shock for the new arrivals. Already the area where the psychedelics lived had begun transforming. They were building it into a peaceful and sustaining area. They had made some requests that she had been a bit concerned about at first, but it all seemed to be working out beautifully for everyone.

Turning her attention back to the boat, she just hoped that today would go smoothly, without any major hiccups. Please let this be a smooth transition. No bad things. Absolutely no bodies!

She watched as the first group made their way toward her. Curiosity was the main emotion she read on their faces. A few of them had nothing except the clothes on their backs, while others each had a small bag of belongings. She welcomed them warmly as they passed by her, some responding in kind and others ignoring her.

One exceptionally large man stopped in front of her, eyeing her hungrily up and down. "Name's Ron. Are you one of the perks of this place? Come find me later and I will give you the ride of your life, or we could just do it right here. I don't mind putting on a show for everybody."

Cheeks flushing angrily, Olivia snapped. "It would be in your best interest to keep moving and get signed in. This is your one and only warning."

"Haha, the kitten has claws. I will be seeing you again, pussycat," the man said, continuing the walk up to the building after one last sweeping look over her body.

Flustered and angry, Olivia looked down at her clothing, knowing that it was professional and not at all provocative. She wondered how people could be such classless lumps of flesh. She should be able to wear whatever she wanted and not have to worry about some low-life jerk making comments that made her feel uncomfortable about her clothing choices. She made a mental note to get that guy's name and make sure to get the information and what happened over to Sari so the security team could keep an eye out for this individual.

Moving to greet the final group of incoming people, Olivia noticed that the woman last in line looked somewhat familiar: curvaceous body and long blonde hair, wearing shorts and a skimpy tank top, apparently the only thing that she owned. The closer she got, the more Olivia realized that she must know her from somewhere, the realization suddenly dawning on her.

The last time that she had seen this woman, she was standing naked in someone's front yard. High as a kite, she had pissed all over Dave's brand-new jacket that Olivia had tried to cover her with.

Believing that this woman, Sabrina, could not possibly remember her, Olivia addressed her as she had all the others that had come through.

She followed the group inside to see how things were progressing. Dave looked up, seeming to count the number of people left to sign in, but then his eyes stopped on Sabrina, and a look of shock crossed his face when he recognized her. He gathered his composure quickly, continuing his work, throwing quick glances at her occasionally. Most of the people in this group seemed to have buddied up with others.

Sabrina was different. She stood off to the side alone, gazing over the crowd of people, weighing and measuring them. It was like she was deciding who she wanted to pair up with. In that moment, Olivia realized that Sabrina was both intelligent and manipulative. She would need to keep a close eye on her.

As though she could feel Olivia's eyes upon her, Sabrina turned and met her gaze, her own unwavering, and gave her a cocky half smile. She leaned back against the wall and tilted her head up, almost seeming to challenge Olivia to come over to her.

Ignoring Sabrina's body language, Olivia stopped by Dave's desk to do a quick check to find out the name of the man that she'd had the unpleasant encounter with earlier. After gathering his information, she decided to skip right over to Sari in security, instead of going to the health center as originally planned.

Upon reaching the security headquarters, Olivia found Sari deep in conversation with one of her guards, going over some footage from one of the many cameras on the island.

"Everything alright, Sari?"

Turning and looking over her shoulder, she replied, "I think so. We seem to have had some late-night activity on one of the beach areas. I just wanted to review the footage and make sure that we don't have anyone trying to get on or off island without permission."

"Lovely. What did you find out?"

"From what we can gather, a few people went to the shore to party and do some Ink together. Some left and went back home, but a couple stayed and went out into the water, which triggered the alarm. So, Lance went out to find out what was going on."

"Good job with the quick work, Lance. What did you find when you got to the beach?"

"Well, it was fairly innocent, I believe. They were, umm, on the edge of the water having sex when I got there. I didn't watch them or anything, but I stayed near them to make sure they didn't end up in trouble in the water. After they finished, I informed them that part of the contract stated that beach areas were off-limits after dark and sent them on their way."

"Great, we certainly don't want anybody drowning! We also don't want to interfere with their personal lives. It would have been alright if you had interrupted them since they were breaking protocol."

"Yes, ma'am."

"Thank you, Lance, you may go now," Olivia said, watching the young man walk away, confidence in his stride. "Sari, I came over to give you some information on a couple of our new residents. One of them is a man that I had some words with when he first arrived. He offered me the ride of my life. So disgusting. The other is our friend Sabrina from my hometown."

"Sabrina? I don't remember that name."

"Seriously, Sari? She pissed all over Dave's jacket!"

"No shit! She's here? Well hell, it's a small world, isn't it? It doesn't really surprise me, though. I will give their information to my people and have them keep an eye out."

"I don't think we have to worry so much about with Sabrina, but that guy, Ron, he seems aggressive and confrontational. He doesn't seem to understand the meaning of the word 'no.' I don't want any of the female workers or residents feeling unsafe. One wrong move and he will be back on the mainland and in jail."

"Which housing area is he in, and is it coed?"

"He was placed in area five with the other men."

"Alright, I will handle it. You doing alright, Liv? You seem a little tense today."

"Yeah, I'm alright, I was just worried about these guys coming to-day. Some of them won't really want to be here, I'm sure. Everything just seems to be going so well, I can't help but feel like something big, and probably bad, is about to happen."

"If you need a distraction, I can come over after work tonight and take your mind off of everything," Sari suggested with a lavish wink and a flick of her tongue over her lips.

"Yes, please come over after work. I would like to spend some time with you. It's been a while since we really hung out. I miss it, and you. Have you been spending a lot of time with Ameera?"

"Liv, why do you have to ask me these things? No, not lately. I'm probably going to have to become a nun soon. It's been so long that I may have forgotten how to please a woman."

Doubled over with laughter, Olivia said, "I highly doubt that you forgot anything, and sex isn't the only thing that matters in life."

"It's not the only thing, but it certainly adds spice and makes it better."

"I have more important things going on right now. Sex is the least of my concerns. We're hoping for approval to start building more housing sites as long as this next group settles in well and there are no major issues. So our capacity is going to grow even more, which means more people to be responsible for. Speaking of growth, have you been by the psychedelics housing sites? They are doing some amazing things with the land. They have started gardens, and I think one of them has even been weaving baskets for everyone. Bailey came to see me and asked about getting seeds for the gardens. She seems to be the spokeswoman for their group."

"And to think you didn't want them here."

"I still don't believe that they should be here, but I have no choice in the matter, so I may as well embrace the positives of it. As long as everyone gets along, all should be well."

"I've noticed groups forming and have been keeping an eye on that. It seems alright for now, but if they start building some sort of rivalry, then we'll have to step in and make some changes. Are we still doing music at the community center this Friday evening?"

"I believe so. Last time I talked to Zek, he said that he had everything set to move forward. We will need added security that night for the event. I just hope that it is received well, and that we don't have any issues arise because of it."

"There isn't any alcohol available to the residents, so it isn't like they are going to get drunk and rowdy."

"That is absolutely true. I just can't seem to shake this feeling of impending doom. I feel like a little dark cloud has been following me around since I've been back on the island. I have no solid proof that anything bad is going to happen. I just can't seem to shake the feeling."

"Come here. Maybe you just need a good hug." Pulling Olivia in and holding her tight, Sari stroked her hair, murmuring, "That feels nice, right?"

Allowing herself to lean into the embrace, Olivia closed her eyes and let herself feel the connection that the two of them shared. Her body began to relax a bit. "Yes, it is very nice, but we are on the clock."

Shifting to let go, Sari accidentally brushed her hand across Olivia's breast, making contact with her nipple, causing it to become erect. A quiet gasp came from Olivia's mouth. Not saying anything, Sari continued to hold on until Olivia relaxed in her embrace, for once not having to be the strong one. Sari lifted Olivia's face with a finger under her chin and said, "I know we are on the clock, but just let me off this one time." She moved slowly in until their lips were just a breath apart. "You have to say you want me to kiss you, Liv. Remember what I told you in your hallway."

Breath shallow in her chest and lips so close together, Olivia was feeling so many things all at once. The most shocking of all of them was desire. It was not as strong as it used to be, but it was for sure there, a slight fire burning within. "We can't," she whispered, pulling away slowly.

Sari moved away, giving Olivia her space to process what she was feeling. She clearly knew that Olivia was going to bolt as soon as she set her mind straight.

"Umm, I have to get over to the health center and speak with Ameera to make sure everything is running smoothly. I, uh, I will see you tonight, alright?" Walking out of the door as quickly as she could without being completely rude, and with her stomach full of butterflies, Olivia noticed something that she hadn't felt in years: a dampness in her panties. In a confused haze she wondered, *why now?*

28

Lightning ran in long lines across the sky. Thunder rumbled deep and loud as the dark clouds began to move across the ocean toward the island, bringing the promise of heavy rain. She watched the storm roll in slowly, waiting for Sari to arrive for dinner. The feeling in the air was perfectly relatable to the feelings that she was having inside of herself, electric and unsettled. The scent of roasted meat and veggies wafted through the air from the Crock-Pot, warmed and ready to eat. Olivia was thankful that she didn't have to do much work to prepare it with all that was on her mind. Being ever organized, she often had meals in freezer bags prepped ahead of time, so she could just toss them in the Crock-Pot and walk away and still come home to a healthy meal. In this case she threw two bags in the crock to account for the additional person.

She still couldn't let go of the worry that continued to roll around in her mind. That dark cloud taunting her. It seemed to be a warning that something was coming, but it wasn't giving a clue as to what it could be. There was the incident with Sari earlier today, that desire, even as small as it had been, that shook her world to its core. She had told Sari that she wanted to hang out, nothing sexual. Then she had gone and gotten close to her like that, waking a sleeping desire that she had thought was gone for good after two years of silence. She had no idea why it suddenly awoke inside of her, and with Sari, her best friend of all people.

Leaning over the balcony banister, Olivia looked at the island, Euphoria, and took in its beauty. No matter what else may happen, she knew that she had done a good thing here. The coming storm only added to the beauty of the island for her. The trees swaying in the wind, the scent of rain in the air, the electricity adding energy to this place, this sanctuary.

A sanctuary not only to humans, but to cats as well, according to an exciting email that she had received late in the afternoon. She was to have a cat sanctuary here at the community center, to help the residents with emotional traumas or just to relax. The local rescue was going to send its least likely to be adopted over, to give them a purpose and a loving home. It would help to keep the rodent population down as well, which in her eyes was a huge benefit.

Checking the time, she wondered where Sari could be since she was supposed to have been there a half hour earlier. Getting herself another glass of wine, she sat on the balcony, letting the wind blow her hair around, not worried about her appearance now that she was off the clock and knowing that Sari would be the last person in the world to judge her for being a mess both figuratively and literally. She leaned her head back against the chair, allowing her eyes to drift closed. Listening to the thunder and the wind howl, she welcomed the incoming storm. She wanted it to wash over her, to cleanse and renew her energy.

She was so lost in her inner vision of the storm that she didn't hear Sari knock or let herself in. Pulled out of her daydream by the sound of a wine glass being placed on the balcony table, Olivia slowly opened her eyes. She glanced over to see her beautiful friend sitting there, legs crossed, still wearing her suit from work that day, sipping on wine pensively.

"What's going on, Sari? You only have that look when something is or could go wrong. Plus, you're late, a rare occurrence with you."

"I had so many plans for tonight, but talking shop was not one of them. We may have a problem, but I'm not entirely sure yet."

Olivia asked, "What is the possible issue and is there a quick solution to it?"

"I'm not sure about a quick solution because I am not sure it's an issue yet. We've been keeping an eye on a boat that has been somewhat close to shore. Not close enough to raise the alarms, but it seems to be watching or checking out the island. There are signs on the island that clearly state that this is government property and that there is no trespassing allowed. The boat stays just far enough out to be left alone. There are downriggers on the boat, so it could just be fishermen, but I don't think that's the case. This is the third time that we have seen this particular boat in the past month, and we have never seen it hauling in nets or fish."

Concerned now, Olivia sat straight up in her chair. "What do you think it's doing here?"

"I believe that it's feeling the island out for weak spots. Possibly trying to find a way onto the island or a way to get someone out. I need to go see Dave about it, find out who he has flagged as a possible runner. On the other hand, it could be people trying to get on the island to sell drugs since they know that it is chock-full of addicts."

"Yes, but they have no money to purchase anything. They don't need money here."

"They have no money that we know of anyway. I am leaning toward someone trying to figure out how to get someone off the island, but I have no proof or just cause."

"How do you plan on getting proof? I can see it in your eyes, you already have a plan."

"The way I see it, the impending storm will give them cover, especially if it is as bad as they are forecasting it to be. I need to keep eyes on the location of the boat, so that I can make sure that it stays away from shore. They shouldn't be out in this weather. That boat isn't large enough to withstand the waves that will be surging once it hits full force."

"So, if the boat can't withstand the storm, then why in the world are they still out there? What would make someone risk their lives like that?"

"Love, hate, money, all of those things can drive people to madness, Liv. Come on, babe, you know that."

"Yes, I suppose I do. What do you need from me to help with this dilemma?"

"A rain check on dinner, and permission to have a few guards work overtime tonight."

"Of course! We can do dinner at any time, and I'm sure we can have a few guards work overtime for this reason. I will approve it in the system when you turn in the hours. You could also give them extra time off to balance it out if need be."

"Thanks, Liv. Would it be too much to ask if I can come crawl into bed with you once I'm done for the night?" Sari laughed, knowing that the answer would be no.

"I have a better idea! Why don't I come with you to do surveillance? It would be good for me to get out and see how it's done. Besides, it looks bad on me if someone breaches the island, and I want to do my part in keeping that from happening. I can go throw some different clothes on and be ready in no time!"

Sari looked thoughtful, thoroughly pondering the offer of assistance before answering, "Sure, I guess it can't hurt. But out there I am in charge, Liv. I don't want you risking injury or doing anything foolish. I know how headstrong you can be. No arguing with anything that I say, agreed?"

With an excited gleam entering her eyes, Olivia nodded enthusiastically, making for her bedroom to get changed.

Throwing her closet doors open to search for proper spy gear, Olivia embraced the butterflies in her stomach lovingly. Excitement flooded all her senses. She realized that this wasn't really a spy mission, but she didn't care because it still felt so much like a movie. She grabbed black leggings and a black tank top usually reserved for working out. The clothing fit her body like a second skin, making her feel comfortable enough to move freely in case they needed to chase someone or do something else just as dramatic. Giggling to herself, she heard Sari calling from the other room, something about it not being a fashion show and to come on already. Hurrying out the bedroom door, Olivia caught the look that Sari gave her, full of longing and amusement, as she placed the empty wine glasses in the sink.

Shaking her head as they walked down the hall to the stairs, Sari asked, "Where are you going to put your key for the suite in those clothes? You have zero storage in them. Not that I'm complaining about the way they look. On the other hand, those curves could be a bit distracting."

"I have a hidden pocket in the waistband of my pants for the key, and look! They do have pockets!" Olivia said, happily shoving her hands into small slits in the sides of the pants as they made their way out the front door and to the jeep.

Jumping in, she grabbed Sari's hand, saying, "Thank you so much for letting me come with you. I know that you prefer doing your job on your own and it might be silly of me, but this is so exciting. I should be so much more concerned about the possibility of a breach, but I feel like an international spy or something right now."

"I can promise you that spy or security work is not at all exciting. It's pretty boring, but you're welcome. It is nice to see that happy glow on your face again, Liv. It makes it even better that I'm the one that put it there," she responded while putting the jeep in drive and heading for the security center. "I want to see what the radar is picking up and find out where the boat was last seen. I have Lance keeping an eye on it right now through the cameras that we have watching the shoreline. Once I see if it has been on the move or if it is still anchored where it has been for the last few hours, we will head to the area so I can get a closer look."

"We... So we can get a closer look," Olivia joked, winking at Sari as they pulled up in front of the building. "I will wait here."

"I won't make you wait too long," Sari replied, taking Olivia's hand and kissing it gently, leaving Olivia to wonder if the words Sari had chosen were a double-edged sword. Not sure how she felt about that, or the possibility of a physical encounter, Olivia focused on the idea that someone was trying to get to her island illegally.

Olivia felt a new determination surge through her to stop this from becoming an issue. She had worked too hard to build this place from the ground up. She wasn't about to let anything mess this place up now. Euphoria was her brainchild, a way for her to right the wrong that had occurred in her life only a few short years ago.

A short while later, Sari walked with a determined pace out of the building, swinging up into the jeep and gunning the throttle, heading for the south shoreline of the island. "Are they still anchored in the same spot?" Olivia questioned.

"Yes, from what Lance has seen they haven't moved at all. He said that he couldn't even see where anyone had come up on deck. Of course, it is possible that they did, just on the other side where the cameras cannot reach."

"So, what's your plan then? The storm is almost here, I don't understand why they haven't headed for safety somewhere. The ocean is a dangerous place to be in a thunderstorm."

"That's why I am concerned that they are trying to use the storm as cover to get on land or get someone off. We have all the systems up and running, but if the power fails, there will be a short blackout before the backup generators kick on and get everything back online."

"That sounds like a serious flaw in the system. Why wasn't that brought to my attention sooner so that it could be fixed?"

"There isn't much that you can do to fix it, and we didn't think that it would ever become an issue. Most people aren't foolish enough to be sitting in a boat in the ocean during a storm that is bad enough to knock power out. It's basically a death wish to be out there in a small vessel."

"What happens if they hail the island and ask to dock in our port for safety reasons?"

"We are a government facility. We don't let anyone dock in our port. We have hailed them and reported that they are close to trespassing and that they need to be on their way. We also warned them of the storm. They did not respond to either transmission. We have already alerted the Ocean Guard. They will send an available unit when they have one. Here we are. We need to walk the rest of the way. We will be down by the edge of the trees where we can observe them. Grab those binoculars from the glove box so you can help me keep an eye out."

Thunder rumbled loud and strong through the sky as they made their way down a sand and stone path. The air was heavy and threatening. Large drops of water began to fall, making the path slippery, the trees wet and not easy to hold on to for support. Sari's walkie-talkie crackled. It was Lance seeing if they'd made it to their vantage point and reporting that the boat was still in the same spot.

The rain suddenly came pouring down, like buckets being released all at once, making visibility nearly impossible. Olivia grabbed Sari's hand so she didn't get separated from her. Lightning flashed through the sky, bright and bold, making it look like the sun was out for a brief moment, then plunged the world back into the dark wet night. Both soaked to the bone and trying not to fall on the sand and stone, they finally reached the rocky shelf that Sari had set as their lookout point. Luckily for them, there was an overhang that just barely allowed them to set back out of the pouring rain and still see out in the direction that they needed to. Trying to dry her binoculars as much as possible, Olivia took the caps off the lenses and looked out to sea, hoping to find the boat still there. Sari tugged on her arm, pulling her gaze to the right, pointing out to sea at the boat rocking violently in the waves that had begun growing with the storm.

It seemed like they watched the boat forever, just waiting for the sea to swallow it whole while the sky lit up over and over. Their world was consumed with rumbling thunder and beating rain. It was then that Olivia caught sight of a strange movement on the water near the boat as she scanned the horizon. Just a small dark object with a light attached. She strained to see through the driving rain. "Sari look! It looks like someone is climbing up the boat from the water!"

"Son of a bitch!" Sari said, grabbing her mic and shouting into it at Lance. "Check the south-quadrant cameras for the last hour and see if anyone made it ashore. It looks like someone in scuba gear is getting back on the boat right now. Contact Gail in housing and have her account for all the residents ASAP!"

"Do you really think they made it to shore? Maybe they were just diving off the coast looking for a shipwreck or something," Olivia said, not believing her words, even as she was saying them. She felt awful for Sari, knowing that her friend was feeling like she'd failed somehow.

"It's fine. I will investigate it tomorrow and see if any damage has been done," Sari grumbled as she watched the boat speed away, making a note of the direction that it went.

Reaching out, Olivia pulled Sari to her, holding on tight, and pressed her lips to Sari's mouth gently. Sari allowed the kiss for a moment but then moved away quickly.

"Sari?" Olivia called out, confused.

"Now isn't the time or place for this. I have a job to do and so do you," she replied gruffly, leaving Olivia with the sting of rejection even though she knew that Sari was right. It didn't make her feel any better though as she followed her back to the jeep with her head down.

29

Preparations for the night out were in full swing, with almost every employee gathered at the community center to help set up the evening's festivities. Zek was in his element, making sure that everything was in the exact place he envisioned it to be and delegating tasks. He hoped to impress Olivia with the event so that they would be able to continue to run community events such as this on Euphoria on a regular basis.

Olivia watched as her people bantered happily back and forth, the excitement electrifying the air. A contented warmth flowed through her, knowing that she had made the correct choices in hiring these people, loving how they fit together like a family now after a couple of months on the island. Much like every family, they had their quirks and their arguments, but things always went back to being steady and stable.

Glancing over at Sari and her crew made Olivia lose a touch of that contentment, thinking back to the other evening, the kiss, and the abrupt way that it had ended. She still had no idea what had gone wrong, if she had done something to upset Sari or what the issue was. It left her confused and sad because she had thought it was what Sari wanted, and she had been ready to give her a piece of herself. The next day, Sari had been her usual sarcastically comedic self, acting like nothing had happened the previous evening, which only perplexed Olivia even more. Looking at Sari's flawless ebony skin, the confident way she moved enticed Olivia. Sari's strength and suppleness was evident as she made her way around to all the security checkpoints, making Olivia's skin flush with a heat that spread through her body and perplexed her. She wondered if she would ever get the opportunity to figure it out now that Sari seemed so far away.

Attempting to pull herself out of her heated daydream, Olivia made her way over to Zek to see where he felt they were in their preparations. Seeing him so attentive to each detail was a comforting sight, given the possibility of chaos at this event. She wasn't sure what exactly to expect from the crowd of residents, or if they would even show up to listen to the music. If they did, she wasn't sure if they would be high on Ink or not.

She had spoken to Bailey, the spokesperson for the psychedelic group, early the previous morning, so she knew that they would be attending. She knew that there would be no problem with that group, as they were as peaceful as a group could be. She loved what they were doing here on the island, and she was trying to give Bailey most of what she requested from the office, whether it be seeds or fabric.

Bringing her focus back to Zek, Olivia waved and called out to him. "Hey, boss man."

"I don't know about being the boss man, but I sure am enjoying my job today. How are you, Miss Titos?"

"I am well, Zek. How are you? It's been a while since you've gone home. Your husband must be missing you something fierce! Although I am quite happy with all the progress that you have made here over the past couple of months."

"It has been quite some time. I am riding the ferry tomorrow once everything is cleaned up from the event. I put in for a few days off so Tom and I can catch up and have some time together. It makes me happy to hear that you are pleased with my work. Have you heard anything from the RED on their thoughts about how Euphoria is performing?"

"Not yet, but we have an inspection coming up next week. They are sending a combined RED and NED team over to make sure everything is running as it should be and that I am properly doing my job."

"I am sure that you have nothing to worry about. You've made this place into a sanctuary for the lost. The community structures being built here are simply amazing. Have you been by the psychedelics housing area? It is breathtaking, and the way that they include everyone on the island, trying to get them involved with their project is fantastic."

"I haven't been by there in a while. I will have to make a point to visit soon. How is everything here? Do you have everything you need to make tonight run smoothly?"

"I believe so. I just have to go over some security protocols with Sari. Then we should be all set to welcome the people when they arrive later tonight."

At the mention of Sari's name, Olivia blushed, her mind racing back to the feeling of their bodies pressing so close together. Her breath catching, she cleared her throat. "I will get out of your hair then. I need to go check in with Dave at the intake center to make sure that he has the dock all set for the outgoing ferry tomorrow."

"Alright, see you later at the show," Zek said, smiling and looking over her shoulder. "Hey Sari, I have a couple of things I need to see you about. Glad you came over."

Fixing a smile on her face, Olivia turned around to see Sari standing a mere foot away. "Hello. How is security looking for the event tonight?" Olivia asked.

A slight hesitation came over Sari's face. "Everything is in top shape. My crew is ready to go. Don't worry, Liv, tonight will be perfect."

"I don't expect perfection. There is no such thing. See you guys later," Olivia said with a hint of sadness in her voice. The short walk to the jeep seemed to take forever, and the urge to look back and see if Sari was watching her walk away was almost too much to ignore, but she managed somehow. She hopped into the vehicle and drove the five miles to the intake building, where she found only Claudia when she walked through the door.

"Hey Olivia, what brings you down here?" Claudia asked happily.

"I came to see Dave, to make sure he has everything set for the ferry arrival and departure tomorrow. Is he around?"

Looking a little guilty, Claudia hedged. "He was here, but he had to run out for a minute. I made sure that everything was in order. No worries at all."

"Claudia, where did he have to go? It's still fairly early and he should be here now."

Frowning slightly while clearly trying to decide how much to share with her superior and not wanting to betray Dave's trust, Claudia replied, "I'm not exactly sure of the time, but he should be back soon."

Olivia's brows furrowed as she frowned deeply. "What are you covering up, Claudia? I can assure you that it is not worth risking your job for. This is a particularly important evening and if something goes wrong, not only will I be upset, but the entire island could also be in jeopardy."

"I'm sorry, Olivia. It's just that he finally seems better. He was so depressed for a while and nothing that I did or said would cheer him up. About a week ago he started going running during lunch and suddenly he seemed so much happier. So, I just told him that whenever he feels the need to go for a run, it's cool and I will hold down the office. I didn't mean to hide it from you. I just don't want to see him get in trouble since he finally seems like he is coming out the other side of the depression that hit him after he and Tammy split up."

"Alright, so what you are telling me is that you have been doing his work and yours this past week so that he can be happy?"

Olivia's heart went out to the woman as she watched a distraught look move across her face, along with a realization that he, maybe wittingly, was taking advantage of her. "You're falling for him, aren't you?" she asked Claudia gently.

Shrugging her shoulders, she replied quietly, "I'm not sure about falling for him, but I do care for him quite a lot."

"Have you told him how you feel about him yet?"

"No. I'm afraid that things will be awkward if he rejects me since we are always here in the office together. Besides, I don't know if he would go for someone my size."

"What? Claudia! You are a beautiful woman with an amazing personality and a huge heart. What's not to like, sweetheart?"

"I don't know. I guess I'm worried about him thinking that I am unattractive. Tammy was really thin and athletic looking. I'm none of those things. Even though I've lost weight since I've been here, I still don't like the way I look. Regarding the event though, I really do have everything under control. I have been watching and working with Dave for so long now that I can do his job and mine if needed. Not that I want to. It's a lot of work to do both."

"You should never have to do both jobs. That is why there are two of you in this department. Aside from that, I think that you should take some time to figure out how you feel about Dave and how to make sure that it doesn't interfere with your job. I think that you are a beautiful and kind woman. Anyone would be lucky to call you theirs."

"I appreciate that, Olivia. I hope that I can see what you see in me someday."

"I hope so too. I'm pleased that everything is all set for the ferry. You do know that I will be speaking with Dave about his absence today, right? I will not bring you or what you have told me into it. However, he is being paid to be here, so he needs to be working."

"I understand. Thank you for being so understanding."

"I'm heading back to my office for now. I have paperwork to finish before returning to the community center for the event tonight."

Smiling encouragingly at Claudia as she walked out the door, Olivia wondered where Dave could be running off to. She knew that he could not possibly be going running that often, every day. Her mind tossed around many possible scenarios as she drove back to her office, wishing that she could just talk to Sari about it to bounce ideas back and forth.

That would be uncomfortable now though. For whatever reason, the tension between them had gone from playful and comforting to silent and awkward. Something that Olivia never expected would happen to them. Sari was her best friend, her rock, the one that she knew would always be there no matter what the circumstances. She decided right then and there to find out what the issue was and address it immediately before it caused any more damage to their friendship. Tonight. She would find her, corner her if need be, and get this mess resolved.

After hours at her computer while going through emails, filling out requisition forms, dealing with complaints, and trying to figure out a family visitation day for the island, Olivia finally made her way to her condo to get changed for the festivities that evening. Going through her closet, she struggled to find something that would look professional to the crowd, but not office professional.

Her goal tonight was to blend in a little with the island residents and get a feel for how they were doing. She wanted to know how they felt about life on the island. What could possibly go wrong? She immediately regretted that line of thought because in reality so many things could happen to make tonight a failure.

Sighing and hoping for the best, she slid a comfortable aqua-colored cotton sundress over her head, the material lightly clinging to her curves, but not so much that it could be considered provocative. She turned and twisted in front of the mirror to make sure that she didn't have any panty lines showing. She opted to go braless so she wouldn't have straps hanging out and look tacky. Her breasts, full but perky, looked great in this dress, as did the rest of her curves, her body sculpted and fit from consistent workouts.

Her thoughts drifted to Sari, wondering what she would think when she saw her, if she would be tempted or turned off. She wasn't sure now. It was such strange ground to traverse, given that before the incident, she always knew what Sari was thinking, or at least she thought she did. Maybe she had always been wrong, assuming she knew, when she really didn't have a clue. Looking at the time, she saw that the festivities were supposed to start in thirty minutes. Time for her to get moving and head to the community center. With a last peek in the mirror and a toss of her long dark hair, she headed out the door with high hopes for the evening.

The sun was beginning to set, creating a beautiful backdrop to the festivities. The sky was lit in reds, golds, purples, and oranges.

Olivia leaned against a fence post, watching the crowd gathering. A smile played across her lips. She was thrilled at the number of people that had come. She scanned the crowd for Sari but knew that she was likely bouncing back and forth between security checkpoints. The only people that she hadn't seen other than Sari were Claudia and Dave.

There was a distinct difference in the residents in the crowd, and Olivia was easily able to tell who used Ink and who used psychedelics. They both had such different styles; the psychedelic users usually wore loose-fitting hippie-style clothing, very much in touch with the earth, while the others were mostly in jean shorts and T-shirts or tank tops.

The crowd began to whoop and holler when the music started. She cheered with the crowd as Zek began to play a preselected soundtrack. She was happy to see her crew's hard work paying off in such a fantastic way. The residents seemed happy, people in the crowd mingling, shifting, moving closer to the stage, singing along with the music. Song after song was played, the sky grew dark, and lights were turned on all around the center, adding ambience. She kept watch over the crowd, making sure everyone was doing okay, but also searching for Sari so she could talk to her about their encounter.

Her eyes drifting back and forth across the crowd, she frowned disdainfully as she saw the big guy, Ron, who had been so rude upon arriving here on Euphoria. He currently had his arm wrapped possessively around a slender brunette whose face she couldn't see, tossing warning looks at any other men within sight. Just as Olivia was thinking about how to make sure that a situation didn't arise, she caught a glimpse of Sari walking out of the building and heading in her general direction.

Calculating that Sari was heading to the checkpoint by the pathway back to the housing areas, Olivia made a beeline to cut her off, knowing that there was a small garden area right off of the path where she could speak to her.

Watching her get closer and closer, Olivia stepped out onto the path in front of Sari with a small smile. "Can I talk to you for a moment?"

"I really need to go check on my crew, Olivia. I don't want any mistakes tonight."

Standing firmly in front of her, Olivia said, "It can wait. I need to talk to you. Preferably now please."

Sighing deeply with a look of resignation, Sari said, "Fine, what's up?"

"In here," Olivia said, pulling Sari into the small garden. "I want a little privacy. Everything seems fine out there right now."

"Olivia, what is so important that it can't wait? I have a job to do, and you know it."

"What happened, Sari? What did I do wrong that made you rush away from me the other night? I have a right to know."

"Are you serious? You need to discuss that right now? Come on, Olivia, just let it go."

"No, I won't just let it go. You are my best friend. I kissed you. I am sorry if that fucked things up between us for a minute, but I do not want to lose our friendship. Just tell me what I did wrong."

"You didn't do anything wrong. I was mad at myself because of what happened with that boat. You were trying to make me feel better, I got it. The problem is that I do not want you just trying to make me feel better, Liv. I want you to touch me because you want to, because you have the desire to. You can't just get physical with me when you think I need affection to make me feel better. It only makes this dance that we do more difficult."

"I'm sorry. I didn't think about it like that. I can see what you're saying. But I wanted to kiss you. You make me feel all sorts of crazy things lately. I just don't want to risk ruining our friendship. I didn't really start to feel desire again until the other day in your office. Now I feel it every time I look at you. If it is going to get in the way of us being friends, I will just ignore it. I just needed to know if I had done something wrong. Just tell me that we are okay, that our friendship is safe. Please. I need to hear that."

Pulling Olivia in for a close hug, Sari said, "We are fine. Nothing is going to ruin our friendship, so stop worrying about it so much."

Reaching under Olivia's chin and lifting her face, Sari leaned in and kissed her softly, tracing her lips with her tongue. They deepened the kiss and their tongues danced. They got lost in each other, together in the moonlight, their passion building a slow fire between them. Desire began to flood their bodies as soft murmurs and moans were shared. Sari's hand moved to caress Olivia's breast through her dress, bringing her nipples to hard peaks. One hand began a slow journey down over Olivia's firm stomach, wetness pooling between her legs...

A loud shout startled them both and they immediately rushed toward the sound of men arguing. Olivia first saw Ron, fists bunched at his sides, a threatening look on his face, warning another man to stay away from his girl, motioning to a brunette lounging against a nearby tree. Sari instantly rushed in to diffuse the situation. She made quick work of it, the one man heading back toward the music and Ron making his way over to his girlfriend. He stopped near Olivia, giving her a slow look from, head to toe look and saying, "I would trade her for you any day, sexy lady. Whenever you want that ride you just let me know. Maybe we can make it a group thing," he said, winking disgustingly at her while holding his hand out in a gesture to make his woman come to him.

Seeing Sari making her way back to her, Olivia felt relief, until she turned to look at the woman on Ron's arm. Struggling to suck in a breath, her head spinning, Olivia took in the small frame, honey brown hair, smooth complexion, and golden eyes. Shock hit her straight in the gut with such force, she almost fell over and would have if Sari had not caught her first. Her vision blurred as tears welled up in her eyes, breathless from the pain. The thrumming crowd had ceased to exist. It was as though a bubble had formed around the small group. Olivia shook her head, trying to deny what she saw before her. Self-preservation told her to run away as quickly as possible, but her legs didn't seem to work anymore. A body washing up on the island on day one was bad, but this... this was so much worse.

Olivia could speak only one word. "Aria."

"Hello Livia," Aria purred seductively.

Euphoria

Angela Nicole is a high school English Language Arts teacher who finds endless inspiration in both the written and natural worlds. A lifelong lover of reading and writing, she shares that passion through teaching high school English Language Arts. When not in the classroom, she spends her free time surrounded by books, animals, and the great outdoors. Based near the shores of Lake Ontario in Central New York, Angela Nicole recharges by hiking mountain trails, paddling across serene waters by kayak or paddleboard, and is happiest with a good book in hand, a trail underfoot, and a furry friend nearby. Whether in the classroom or out in nature, she is always working on her next story.

9 798218 721282